"What lunatic said, 'Just kiss and make up'?"

Beth: Could this be some kind of delayed empty-nest syndrome? Or maybe she's finally realized she's lost the real Beth—that skinny, unconventional woman with big dreams. Now all she has to do is fly solo, even for just a little while, and find them again.

Howard: As a psychiatrist, he can spot an anxiety attack in a packed mall, but he can't recognize his wife experiencing a full-blown midlife crisis. Howard wants to make Beth happy, but when did the rules of marriage change…and who forgot to tell him?

Kate: As far as Kate's concerned, Beth not only abandoned her father, but the whole family. And *that* is just not acceptable in Kate's well-ordered world. Is image-conscious Kate the only one who can clean up the mess? Or will Beth's freedom shine light on Kate's cracking facade?

Peggy Webb

Peggy Webb is passionate about books, music, theater, gardening, her family, her friends and her dog. When she's not writing, she's either clipping roses in one of the gardens she designed and planted, acting on stage at her local community theater in roles such as M'Lynn Eatenton in *Steel Magnolias*, singing in her church's choir, at her vintage baby grand playing blues, visiting children in far-flung places or laughing with friends. She also writes screenplays, serves on Tupelo's Film Festival committee and claims to make the best walnut bread in two states (Mississippi and Alabama).

This native Mississippian launched her career with a book that hit number one on romance bestseller lists and earned her the Waldenbooks Bestselling New Author Award. Since then, her more than fifty novels have consistently appeared on bestseller lists and won national awards.

She shares her love of books with her students at Mississippi State University as well as lecture audiences throughout the U.S., and she shares her home with the perfect male—her dog.

THE Next NOVEL™

To Nancy –

Flying Lessons

PEGGY WEBB

Happy reading!

Peggy Webb

FLYING LESSONS
copyright © 2006 Peggy Webb
i s b n 0 3 7 3 8 8 0 9 2 8

This edition published by arrangement with Harlequin Books S.A.

TheNextNovel.com

 HARLEQUIN®

PRINTED IN U.S.A.

From the Author

Dear Reader,

When I started writing this book, the Gulf coast of my beloved Mississippi was a sun-kissed spot of beach villages and sea glass and charm. Hurricane Katrina destroyed all that, leaving thousands of people stripped of homes, schools, churches, businesses and most of all, loved ones.

But Katrina has not destroyed hope. Mississippians are a staunch, proud people who know how to rise from the ashes. My son is one of the thousands of emergency personnel who will spend the next year rebuilding the towns and villages.

The Gulf coast in *Flying Lessons* is the one in our memories.

It is my tribute to the courage and resilience of all those who suffered loss and to the compassionate spirit of all those who came to their aid.

As a thank-you to my loyal fans, I'll be giving away book bags for *Flying Lessons*. Go to www.peggywebb.com for contest details.

Sincerely,

Peggy Webb

In memory of Daddy,
my hero against whom all others are measured.

PART ONE

CHAPTER 1

"If this is my life, I want a refund."
                                        —Beth

I don't look like the kind of woman you'd think would run away from home. But here I am in Huntsville, Alabama, wishing I could stamp *Cancelled* on my marriage license and go off somewhere and become somebody else—anybody except Elizabeth Holt Martin, boring, dowdy wife of Dr. Howard Martin.

This strange restlessness is partially why I drove one hundred and fifty miles and paid five hundred dollars to listen to a woman with three degrees and an overbite tell me how to cope with my life. Glenda Wiggs is her name, B.S., M.S., Ph.D., heavy on the B.S.

"Or-gan-ize." She stretches her words, either to lend weight and credibility or to work up a sweat so she won't freeze in this room where the air conditioner is turned up cold enough to kill hogs. "You must keep lists."

She sounds just like my husband. I could have stayed home and saved my money.

"*Pri-ori-tize!*" Wiggs shouts.

I wonder where she would put, *Resist the urge to stand in the aisle at Wal-Mart in front of the Tampax display, cursing your dried-up eggs?* I did that last Tuesday, and Howard asked if I wanted him to write a prescription for Prozac. He's a psychiatrist, which says it all. He can spot a patient having an anxiety attack in a packed mall, but he can't recognize a wife in midlife crisis at Wal-Mart—let alone a wife having an attack of lust in his own bedroom.

Last weekend, in a last-ditch effort to get Howard to notice me, I tossed my panties on the bedpost.

"Elizabeth," he said, "there's a hole in your underwear."

"That's not a hole, Howard. They're *crotchless*."

I didn't even get an acknowledgment from him, much less a rise. The salesgirl at Naughty but Nice had said they were guaranteed to work. Obviously, the panties were flawed.

Of course, you have to consider Howard. He wears two-piece pajamas to bed and then folds them into thirds every morning, even when they're dirty and he's going to put them in the laundry hamper. I used to love Howard's sense of order and neatness, but lately I've wanted to take his precisely folded, accusatory pajamas and stomp them. Instead, I refold them into sloppy halves, toss them back under the pillow and say, *There, take that.*

I don't know what's wrong with me. My Lord, I'm fifty-three and my older daughter, Kate, left the nest ten years ago. Of course, my late-in-life child, Jenny, will be leaving for college this fall, so technically I could be suffering delayed empty-nest syndrome. But it's more than that, I think. I feel like somebody who got all dressed up for the parade and by time I got there, it had already passed by.

Sitting here, on a hard chair in the Imperial Room at the Marriott on Tranquility Base, I forget about folded pajamas and failed panties. Instead, I look out the window at the Saturn Five rocket dominating the Space Center, thrusting toward the wide open spaces, grand and glorious and phallic.

Wouldn't I love to get on that and ride? I'd go straight to the moon—both ways. I'd forget that my nest is empty, my eggs are dried up and my husband can't find the henhouse.

We don't even have conversations anymore. He hasn't started one with me in three years that doesn't begin with, "Elizabeth, where are my…?" Fill in the blank. "Where are my gray socks, my car keys, my reading glasses, my hemorrhoid suppositories?"

Who am I trying to kid? It's not Jenny's exodus to college I mind. It's not even creeping age, missing car keys and socks. It's sex. I can't remember the last time Howard and I had sex.

"Beth…" My friend Jane startles me out of my reverie. She's the only person who calls me by my childhood nickname. I'd love her for that alone, but she's also full of every good thing I can imagine—kindness, truth, laughter, loyalty and love. She's like a Mars bar brimming with nuts and marshmallows and caramel and chocolate. Once you get a taste of Jane Meaders, you don't let her go.

I glance around the cold room where women are milling about talking in that too-sweet drawl Southern women use when they're telling lies under the guise of being polite. Jane has turned sideways in her chair and is giving me a funny look. "Are you having another hot flash?"

"No. I don't have hot flashes. I just sweat a little at night, is all."

"Same thing." Jane's nine years older than I am, and thinks of herself as my mentor in all things female, which covers everything from menopause to self-exams for breast cancer to how to remove rust rings from the bathtub. Which is fine by me. When you don't know where you're going, it's good to have a best friend who has already traveled the road.

"Let's get out of here," she says. We hurry toward the parking lot without looking back and without one iota of guilt. If there's one good thing about being over fifty, it's the ability to leave in the middle of a boring lecture without being labeled bad-mannered. What people think is *weak bladder*.

We toss our purses into the backseat of Jane's new silver Sequoia, and she says, "Whose idea was this anyway, yours or mine?"

"Howard's."

"Well, that explains it. Which way's the mall?"

I hate malls—too many three-way mirrors—but I check the map, anyhow, because Jane loves to shop. As we head toward University Drive, I forget about having an itch Howard won't scratch. Spring takes my breath away. I've always said, "May in Mississippi can make you weep." The same is true of Alabama or Georgia or any other state in the Deep South. Mother Nature puts on such a show of greenery and blossom, it looks as if she's trying to compensate for all the tornadoes she sends our way. Creeping purple phlox hides the raw red-clay hills, wisteria cascades from magnolia trees in sweetly scented curtains, and the fragrance of wild honeysuckle spilling over fences makes you drunk on happiness for no reason at all. Gardens riot with explosions of golden forsythia, parades of iris in white and yellow and blue, and arbors bending under the weight of climbing pink roses.

I almost say, "Jane, it's too pretty to be indoors. Let's head straight to the botanical gardens." I don't though. Somewhere between the ages of twenty and fifty I turned into my timid aunt Bonnie Kathleen.

In college I was going to be Edna St. Vincent Millay, compose great symphonies instead of poetry and live a wild, rich bohemian life that would be as far removed from Aunt Bonnie Kathleen's vision for me as possible. She's the maiden aunt who raised me. My mother died in childbirth, and Daddy, unable to cope with the loss and a baby girl at the same time, left me in the care of his only sister. Aunt Bonnie Kathleen dished out love and discipline in equal but cautious doses. Her idea of keeping me in line was the dire warning, "I swear, Elizabeth, if you wear that red dress (or cut your hair, or drive that car or do whatever else she didn't want me to do), I'm going to have a prostration attack." It worked, not because I feared that bogus malady but because I couldn't bear to hurt her feelings.

Eighteen and newly freed from the strict eye of Aunt Bonnie Kathleen, I wore gypsy skirts and purple lipstick, wrote a song called "Love is a Bus" and spouted radical opinions. Once, I danced naked on the balcony of the Tri Delta house while I ate cherries from a jar. Now I wear Martha Stewart–like clothes, copy recipes from *Good Housekeeping* and worry that I've lost the real Beth—that skinny, unconventional woman with the big dreams—somewhere along the way.

Well, certainly I've lost *skinny*. Last week while Howard was snoring on his side of the bed and I was tossing and burning on the other, I sneaked into the kitchen and ate peanut butter from the jar. All of it.

That's why I hate stores with three-way mirrors. Even Ann Taylor, Jane's favorite.

"One of the compensations of growing old," she says as we bypass the bargain rack and select from the new arrivals without even checking the price tags. "Fat pocketbooks."

"Fat behinds."

"Beth, you're not fat. Trust me. At a certain age, the weight shifts."

"How come it didn't shift to my breasts where I needed it?"

"Gravity." She should talk. Jane's tall and elegant, a perfect size eight. She grabs a blue dress off the rack and thrusts it toward me. "Here, try this one on. It looks like you."

I squeeze into the dress, which matches my eyes.

"Buy it. The blue makes the gray streaks in your hair look like blond highlights," Jane says. The trick to being a good friend is knowing when to make you feel better with a lie and when to shake some sense into you with the truth. This is a feel-good lie.

"It's too small. Since when did they start making size twelves this small?" I complain.

"They're skimping on material. Let's get an ice-cream sundae, then head out to the botanical gardens before they close."

Jane's reading my mind—another reason I love her. I guess that's the way it is with friends of thirty years. When I married Howard and moved to Tupelo, a young Gulf Coast bride pining for sea and surf and sand, plopped down in the pine hills of northeast Mississippi where I had to drive twenty miles for the nearest whiff of water, Jane took me under her wing. We met at Village Books where we were both reaching for the same copy of Edna St. Vincent Millay's biography, *Savage Beauty*. She showed me the best place to buy good cuts of rump roast, the church with the best choir and later—after I really got to know her— the best place to do the primal scream. She drove up the Natchez Trace Parkway on the outskirts of Tupelo to a hill overlooking nothing but farmland, then said, "Just let her rip. Nothing but cows to hear."

It's been so long now I can't remember why I went, but that was the only time I ever used the screaming hill. Not because there haven't been plenty of reasons, but because I told myself grown-ups don't act like that: they don't just go around letting emotions rip and scaring cows.

Nowadays, the only time I let my emotions rip is when I'm eating lobster dripping with butter or ice-cream sundaes with lots of nuts and a mountain of whipped cream. Lord knows, I don't get a chance in the bedroom.

Jane eats in silence, but I make humming sounds of pleasure.

In malls, ice cream is always served with plastic spoons that are too small, so it takes us a while to finish. By the time we arrive at Huntsville's Botanical Gardens, we have only an hour left before closing.

The handsome sixtyish man who takes our money looks as if he might have retired from the military. Milton, his name tag reads. He has the cropped close hair and the upright bearing of somebody accustomed to giving and taking orders.

"Senior's discount," Jane says, then hands him three dollars and fifty cents.

"This I don't believe." The smile Milton flashes shows straight white teeth that are either the best dentures I've ever seen or a miracle of nature. "I'll have to see your driver's license."

He's flirting with Jane. Most men do, even thirty-year-olds. When she pulls out her license, he says, "Unbelievable."

I take five dollars out of my purse.

Barely glancing my way Milton says, "Three-fifty, please."

Even if he had looked at me more closely he would probably have said the same thing. Nobody would ever describe me as a beautiful older woman. The most I can hope for is attractive, and that's stretching it.

"I'm fifty-three."

I hand over the five dollars and, for a moment, I think he's going to ask for proof. He takes my money, then waves us through.

"Jackass," Jane mutters when we're out of hearing.

"He's just doing his job."

"Still…"

It's such a small thing, being mistaken for a senior citizen nine years before the fact, but even so I suddenly see my life as a series of small defeats. The concerts I never played, the music gathering dust, even the elementary school carnival that lost money the year I was PTA president.

I used to tell myself I had plenty of time to do whatever I wanted, but I don't do that anymore; I just bury myself in the routine of being Howard's wife, Jenny and Kate's mother, little Bonnie's grandmother and until a month ago, caretaker to Aunt Bonnie Kathleen. My only connection to music is serving on the board of the symphony league…if you don't count the symphony I've been composing off and on for twenty years. More *off* than *on* because I simply can't hear the music anymore.

Jane and I smell the roses before we see them. We round the corner to a profusion of deep red blooms dripping from a wrought-iron arbor.

"I wish mine would bloom like that," Jane says. "Last year I had only fifty roses on my climbing Don Juan."

"I had aphids and black spot blight."

"You should try spraying with soda and liquid detergent mixed in water. I'll give you the formula."

"Umm-hmm," is all I say because I'm snatched inside out by the young couple coming toward us.

The man has a deep tan and the longish kind of hair that looks good windblown, and the young woman, who could be Carly Simon's double except pregnant, is laughing at something he said and holding on to her slightly bulging abdomen. They linger beside a New Dawn climber, kissing, and I picture them in a small apartment where you have to step over the coffee table to get to the bathroom. I imagine them tangled together in a brass bed in broad daylight, breathing each other in, loving in the fierce, jubilant way of people who have their whole lives before them.

When was the last time Howard and I loved like that? When was the last time we left the light on?

I don't even own underwear that matches anymore.

I imagine this young couple's baby coming into the world, a little girl with red hair like her mother's. I picture the young woman bending over the bassinet while her child sleeps, burying her face in the downy hair, inhaling the fragrance of baby powder and innocence.

Jenny's room is losing her fresh sun-and-wind scent. I can't even detect the smell of the damp socks she always used to toss behind her headboard.

Where did all the years go? How did I end up here in the botanical gardens envying two people I don't even know?

Overwhelmed with the scent of roses and loss, I start to cry, not heaving sobs that announce grief in a way that makes people stop and stare, but silent tears that burn a path down the cheeks and evaporate before anybody notices. Anybody except your best friend.

Without saying a word Jane takes my arm and leads me to a bench surrounded by thick ferns and half-hidden among a copse of wise-looking oaks, their ancient trunks covered with lichen, their low-hanging branches saying, *Here, rest awhile*. She digs around in her purse and comes up with a tattered pink tissue, obviously used.

I blow my nose while she waits in Madonna-like patience, hands folded and face carved with concern. A big sigh shudders through me, and I think the tears might start all over again, but they don't.

"Go ahead," Jane urges. "You didn't even cry at the funeral. You're due after what you've been through."

"This is not entirely about Aunt Bonnie Kathleen. She's at peace."

And I am, too, with that part of my past. In her five-year battle with cancer, I was finally able to give back a small portion of the loving care she generously lavished on me.

"Okay, then. Do you want to tell me what's wrong?"

"No...yes. That seminar was awful."

"Yeah, but not that awful." She shoots me a sly look, and suddenly we're grinning, then laughing. In perfect imitation of Dr. Wiggs, Jane says, "Or-gan-ize. Pri-ori-tize."

"Why should women cope?" I ask after we finish our laughter-is-the-best-medicine break. "Why can't we grow wings and fly?"

"Because we have too much ballast to get off the ground?"

"No, really... Don't you ever wish you'd done something different? Don't you ever get the feeling that you've let the important things slip through your fingers?"

"I try not to think too much about it."

Maybe that's my problem. I think too much.

But I don't say that to Jane because the implication is that I'm a deep thinker while she's shallow, which is the exact opposite of the truth. Besides, we'd set out to Huntsville for the express purpose of having a relaxing getaway weekend, in spite of the seminar Howard insisted we book.

And here I am being a wet blanket, ruining our good time.

"Hey, we'll never get through the gardens if we don't hurry."

I reach for her hand, help her up, and we finish our tour arm in arm.

That evening we decide to have supper at the Macaroni Grill, which sounds like a place that serves home-style cooking from a buffet topped with tacky plastic hoods that are supposed to keep you from breathing on the food, but don't. Since we've eaten at the Macaroni Grill in Memphis, we know what to expect: fresh flowers in real Italian pottery, chefs in tall white hats tending a stone oven and the smell of baking bread that makes you forget everything except sitting at a table with a real linen cloth and dipping soft white rolls into garlic-flavored oil.

What I want to order is a wallowing-in-the-doldrums, get-me-knee-walking-drunk whiskey, but since this is a nice upscale restaurant I settle for a lovely, sophisticated Pinot Grigio. The first glass makes me forget about a stale marriage and the second glass makes me forget about lost dreams. By the third glass I've even taken the edge off sex. Or the lack thereof.

"Whoa, Beth. Since when do you drink like that?"

"Since I'm out of town and nosy busybodies can't run tattling."

I'm drifting along in a fog, and my slurred S's sound exactly right.

"Maybe we should order now. You need food."

Jane signals our waitress, a lush, porcelain-skinned young woman, who tells us she's from nearby Decatur and wants to transfer from Calhoun Community College to Memphis State and study opera.

"Then you should do it," I tell her.

I'm feeling wise and worldly, a woman floating above her former frumpy self, transformed into a cross between Solomon and Isadora Duncan. If I had a long silk scarf around my neck I'd dance on the table and twirl it. Instead I wave my arms about in a magnanimous fashion.

"Do it before you're too old," I say. "Do it now! 'Enjoy your ice cream while it's on your plate!'"

In the midst of my Thornton Wilder quote, my flailing arm crashes into a tray loaded with shrimp scampi and fettuccine Alfredo. The waiter sidesteps and tries to hang on to the teetering tray, but it's no match for my Isadora Duncan performance. Noodles and shrimp sail across the room and land on pressed khakis, white shirts and lacquered hairdos. One fat, pink jumbo-sized morsel nosedives into the plunging neckline of a woman twice the size of Texas. Fascinated, I watch her hop around the table and smack her husband on the head with her Gucci handbag.

"You pig!" she yells, as if he had personally and maliciously dumped the shrimp in her cleavage.

"Can you believe she can move that fast?" I ask Jane, but she's too busy settling the bill and hustling me out of the restaurant to reply.

"I wanted ice cream," I tell her.

"Just hush."

When we arrive at the Marriott, I discover I've left my legs at the Macaroni Grill. Jane props me against the side of the car, drapes my arms around her neck like a fox-tail wrap and drags me through the lobby where one of the guests is playing bad country music on the baby grand piano.

"Wait…stop. I know that song. I want to sing."

"Bad idea. Your second of the evening."

"Ha."

My snit lasts until we enter the elevator and lurch toward our third-floor room. "I think I'm going to be sick."

"Not here, you won't."

Jane quells my nausea with a look and then manhandles the stubborn lock on the hotel door without uttering one unladylike word. But when victory is in sight, she wraps my arms around the toilet, then marches out of the bathroom with her back stiff.

I heave up sour wine and regret, and then splash water on my face. I look like the aftermath of Hurricane Camille.

"Jane," I call through the closed door. "Are you mad at me?"

She opens the door and stands there looking like something from the pages of *Vogue* in her red silk pajamas.

"I'm sorry, Jane."

"You look like hell. Can you dress yourself?"

"Yes."

I don't know if that's the truth, but I'm not about to be the source of any more trouble. I struggle out of my clothes and put on an oversize white nightshirt with a slogan that reads, Give In To Your Animal Instincts. I would take the advice of my own nightshirt, but in spite of tonight's performance I don't even know if I have animal instincts. My fear is that thirty years of routine have wiped them out.

Mourning for my extinct animal, I borrow Jane's Mary Kay cream to remove my makeup while she brushes her teeth, and then we both climb into the king-size bed the Marriott gave us instead of two doubles. Lying under the same covers with the sound of a good friend breathing nearby sometimes helps.

Not tonight, though. There's a hole in me that nothing can fill.

We lie there a while in the dark, then Jane says, "What time do you want to go home tomorrow?" Ignoring the real issue.

But I can't. I picture Howard, the Real Issue, at the Radisson Hotel in Jackson, Mississippi, where he's attending a psychiatry seminar, going through files he brought from home, jotting notes in neat, precise handwriting. He's probably glancing at his watch thinking he has one more hour to work before he goes into the bathroom for his fifteen-minute bedtime ritual—brush teeth, floss, wash face, fold his dirty clothes and stow them in the plastic bag in his suitcase, unfold his blue-striped pajamas, which he will wear two nights in a row, maximum.

Next he'll glance at his daily planner to his notation on Sunday, May 25, written in neat block letters. ELIZABETH RETURNS. He'll make a mental note of it, nod, then bury his face back in his files.

For Howard, my homecoming will be just another entry on his schedule, a small deviation from the routine that rules his life.

"Jane...have you ever thought of running away from home?"

Foolish question. Of course, she's never thought of such a thing. She and Jim adore each other. They still hold hands after forty years of marriage.

"Every woman does." Her response both surprises and vindicates me. "At least once in the marriage. I think it comes with the territory."

If she's right, then maybe this notion of taking flight is a passing fancy. Maybe I just need to get home and back to my normal routine. *Oh, help*. Awful, spirit-killing routine.

"I'm not going home."

"You're kidding. Right?"

"No. I'm going back to Tupelo, but not to stay."

"You're stressed out from years of caregiving and the funeral, Beth."

"It's more than that, Jane. I've been thinking about this since Jenny left."

Three days after the funeral, when Howard announced that she was to spend the summer in Tupelo working in his office, she yelled, "You're trying to smother me. I'm not fixing to turn into Aunt Bonnie Kathleen." Then she declared her intention to spend the summer backpacking with friends in Arizona. At that precise moment I thought, *If my daughter can run away, why can't I?*

It's as if Aunt Bonnie Kathleen's death unlocked a dam inside Jenny and me. But while my daughter poured forth her rebellion, I've been mulling it over, mentally testing the waters, vacillating between taking the scary plunge and pulling back to the safety of the dock.

Aunt Bonnie Kathleen left me all her worldly possessions—a 1950s-style cottage in Ocean Springs, a 1979 Oldsmobile Cutlass that hasn't run in seven years, a closet full of hopelessly out-of-date clothes... and a quarter of a million dollars.

Who would have thought it? A modest, small-town public school music teacher. But then, she never spent a penny on herself. Never took a vacation. Never bought a new piece of furniture. Never indulged in a fancy, frivolous party frock—except that one time when she thought Mr. Weems, the high school's assistant principal, was coming for dinner. I'll never forget it. There she was, flush-faced and smiling, all decked out in a new blue taffeta dress with dyed-to-match shoes when he called and claimed his car wouldn't start.

She wrapped the dress in tissue paper and mothballs, put it in the bottom of Grandmother Holt's steamer trunk and never mentioned his name again, just put on that brave smile. If she was hurt or disappointed, nobody ever knew.

Long-suffering. That's what she was. Or maybe she just never imagined a different life for herself.

But I do. I don't hear the music anymore. I want to rekindle the song, reignite my marriage, reinvent myself so that my daughters and my granddaughter will have a role model who is brimming with life and joy and hope. I don't want to die and have them say, *Oh Lord, I hope I never turn into Mother.*

After the reading of Aunt Bonnie Kathleen's will I said to Howard, "Let's take that exotic dream vacation we used to talk about. Let's go to Paris."

"Maybe next year," he said. "After I get a partner to help me look after patients."

I didn't remind him that's what he'd said last year when I suggested going to the Smoky Mountains, or the year before when I mentioned taking a long weekend at the Peabody in Memphis. In fact, I don't remind him of anything anymore. I don't have enough spirit to bother.

We're in the grip of a strange malaise, Howard and I. It's a pattern we've built through the years, and I fear that it will soon be set in stone, if it's not already. I see us sliding into old age, bitter, silent people, shackled together by a legal document...unless I take drastic measures.

I look at Jane. "As soon as I get back to Tupelo, I'm leaving."

I've rendered the unflappable Jane speechless. Now that the bold statement is out there floating in the silence between us, I'm terrified. Do I have the courage to strike out on my own at this age?

We forgot to close the privacy drapes, and through the sheer curtains I can see Saturn Five lit up and pointed straight toward the shiny new moon that hangs over this city of 160,000 people.

"You've had too much to drink," Jane says. "Get a good night's sleep, and in the morning we'll stop in Decatur at the cute little breakfast place on Moulton Street."

"This is not alcohol talking."

She snaps on the bedside lamp, lifts herself on one elbow and stares at me.

"You're serious, aren't you?"

"Yes. I've made up my mind. This is my last chance. If I don't leave now, I'll never get up the courage again."

"What do you want me to do?"

This is what I love most about Jane. She knows when to argue me out of my notions and when to lend unconditional support.

"Just don't stop being my friend."

"I won't."

She turns out the light, and in a little while I hear her soft, even breathing, but I can't sleep. I've just turned my future into a blank page, and I don't even know if I can still write.

CHAPTER 2

"If you're driving your own car,
    are you still running away?"
                                    —Beth

Highland Circle is a posh community where old
money and nouveau riche live side by side in gracious,
shaded lots deep enough for privacy but narrow
enough to have close neighbors. People who move in
tend to stay until they die, which means there's not
much turnover in residents. If you live by a grump,
then you're likely to have to put up with him for the
duration. Fortunately my curmudgeonly neighbor was
eighty when Howard and I bought our sprawling Tu-
dor house, and when his Greek Revival home came
up for sale, I couldn't wait to tell Jane.

The downside of running away is leaving behind a
dear friend who gave me a key to her side door when
she moved here twenty years ago, and has never asked

to take it back, even four years ago when I ran sobbing into her house at midnight because I'd called Howard at the Park Plaza in San Francisco and heard a woman in his room.

Jane gave me a cool washcloth for my face, a cup of hot chocolate for my soul and levelheaded advice for my peace of mind.

"Howard's too orderly to engage in a messy affair. Did you ask who it was?"

"No."

"Call him right now and ask."

When I shook my head, she handed me the phone. "If you don't call him, I will."

The woman turned out to be Brenda Miles, a business associate from Oxford.

"Not only is Brenda in my room," Howard had said, "but also Bob Atterford, Jim Mansfield and Stacy Beckman. We're discussing business. Now are you satisfied, Elizabeth?"

I was satisfied that he wasn't being unfaithful, but unsatisfied in so many other ways that even now the prospect of leaving Jane does not sway my resolve.

And I'm unutterably grateful that it's possible. Many women who feel trapped have the desire but not the means. One of the compensations of age is having your own bank account, your own car and the luxury of time.

Standing in my doorway, Jane says, "You'll call me when you get where you're going, won't you? You'll keep in touch?"

"I will."

I hug her hard then go inside and walk through my house. It has five bedrooms and three baths, so this takes a while. The walls are coordinating shades of blue and beige and every stick of furniture matches. It's as colorless and plain as Aunt Bonnie Kathleen's house in Ocean Springs, as sanitized and predictable as I feel. If this is the image I project, no wonder I can't light Howard's fire.

Maybe I'll go to the Gulf Coast and redecorate the seaside cottage Aunt Bonnie Kathleen left me. I'll paint all the walls purple, and not a single thing will match. I might even buy lamps with red fringed shades.

The thought cheers me up, and I sit at the kitchen table to call Jenny on her cell phone.

"Mom, is that you?" My daughter sounds happy and very far away, her voice brimming with life.

"Yes, honey, it's me. Are you having fun?"

"I'm having a blast. Is everything all right at home? How's Dad? How're you?"

"Dad's traveling. And I just got back from my trip with Jane."

"She's a blast. Is Jacob still engaged to that snooty little witch, Bitsy Lynn What's-Her-Name?"

Jacob is the youngest of Jane's four sons, a brilliant and very fine young man doing his residency in pediatrics at the University of Alabama Medical Center in Birmingham. He broke all our hearts when he fell for a debutante whose goal is the perfect tan and whose major concern is the color of her fingernail polish.

"He is, and you be nice."

"*Nice* would be Kate, not me."

My older daughter *is* nice…and conservative to the bone. Like Howard. Telling Jenny about my decision is going to be a piece of cake compared to explaining my plans to Kate.

"You're nice, too, Jen."

"Daddy thinks I'm wild."

"A little bit of wildness is not a bad thing. It stretches you, lets you grow."

"Wow, Mom. Are you getting hip in your old age?"

"Maybe…listen, honey, I don't want you to be upset, but I've decided to go away for a while."

"Where are you going? Paris? You've always wanted to go there?"

"I don't know yet. I just need to get away from home. Your dad's gone a lot and I need…a little breathing room."

"How long will you be gone?"

How long will it take to turn around a relationship? A life?

"I'm not sure. But I'll call you every day, and you call me on my cell phone if you need me. I mean that, Jen. Anytime. Day or night."

"Mom…you sound so serious." Jen laughs. "I can take care of myself."

"I know, honey."

If I thought she couldn't I wouldn't be leaving, not even to hole up in a motel for a few days, lick my wounds, then crawl back chastened and contrite.

After I hang up, I start to dial Kate but put the receiver back down. The thought of leaving the sweet, dimpled arms of my three-year-old granddaughter, Bonnie, chokes me up. We see each other every week, and between times we talk on the phone. The last time we spoke she told me, "Nana, I love you more than bacon." Bonnie's favorite food is bacon, so that puts me high on the hog.

I don't know how I can leave her.

And maybe I shouldn't. Maybe I'm a foolish older

woman with hormones run amok. Maybe I'm expecting Rachmaninoff's Prelude, opus 3 when I ought to settle for "The Old Gray Mare."

It's not that I'm not grateful for what I have. I *am*. But is it wrong to want more, to long for joie de vivre?

Now I understand why Aunt Bonnie Kathleen lived in one place all her life and never even changed the color of her bedspread. Green. When the old one wore out she bought another one exactly like it.

Change is wrenching. Especially for the timid.

I close my eyes, try to imagine the woodwinds in Sinding's "Rustles of Spring," the piano in Beethoven's *Moonlight* Sonata. But nothing's there. How can you pour love and music out of an empty shell?

Don't I owe it to my family as well as to myself to be the best woman I can be, to be somebody they can look up to?

I grab a pad and pencil before I can change my mind.

Dear Howard,
I need some time away, so I'm leaving for a while and don't know when I'll be back. Please don't try to find me. I'll call to let you know I'm safe when I get where I'm going.

Don't forget to feed the dog. Don't buy that cheap dog food that comes in chunks because Rufus won't eat that. You have to buy the kind that comes in little pieces the size of miniature shredded wheat. I can't think of the brand... And don't wait till evening to feed Rufus because then he won't sleep, and don't forget to water the ferns...

Seeing the long list of minutiae that makes up my day, I suddenly stop writing. Just stop.

I go into the bedroom suite I share with Howard, take down my suitcase and rifle through my ugly dresses, the kind women buy when they're trying to hide their hips.

I slap the dresses, every one of them, then throw my empty suitcase onto the closet floor. I don't want to take a single thing that reminds me of my current life. Next, I rummage on the top shelf till I find what I'm looking for—my long-neglected symphony, the edges of the box crumpled by the weight of winter blankets. Sitting cross-legged on the floor, I lift the lid and stare at the title—*Soaring*.

Can I? Do I still have wings?

I stuff the unfinished symphony into a tote bag

with my underwear and toothbrush, then grab my
purse and walk out, stopping only long enough to
write a different note to Howard.

I'm leaving for a while. I'll call and explain later.
Feed the dog.

Let him figure out the rest for himself.

Although it's already 2:00 p.m., I say goodbye to
Rufus, tell him Howard's in charge but not to forget
how to use the doggie door and the automatic food
dispenser; then I get in my silver Cadillac Seville and
drive off anyway. Now that my decision is made, I
can't stand to spend another night in this empty
house.

I honk the horn when I pass Jane's, knowing full
well she won't peer out the window or come to the
door and wave me off. She hates goodbyes. Right now
she's probably curled into her yellow chintz chaise
longue in her sunroom with her head buried in a book
so she won't see my car cruising down the street.

Truth to tell, I hate goodbyes, too. I wish I had not
honked the horn, but there's no way to take it back.

Instead of wasting time on useless regret, I pick up
the phone to dial Kate, but break out in a sweat at the

thought of telling her. I've never known what to say to her, even when she was three years old. She's just like Howard—cool, self-possessed, completely in charge of her emotions and never needy.

Jane says Kate was born old, but I think I simply abdicated motherhood when she was born. Not that I didn't love her, but I thought Howard knew more about parenthood than I did, and so I sat back and let him take over with Kate.

He'd had two loving, well-adjusted parents and I'd been brought up by a woman whose idea of childhood was "mind your manners, keep your dress clean and don't speak unless you're spoken to."

Aunt Bonnie Kathleen swore by the TV show *Father Knows Best*, starring Jane Wyatt and Robert Young, and I grew up thinking the key to happiness was having a man on the premises. She could have swapped places with Jane Wyatt's character and nobody would have noticed the difference. Since my father didn't live in our household, nobody knew best and my aunt and I just muddled along until I finally found a hero who would take care of both of us.

That would be Howard, who has lately lost his shine.

Kate's house comes into view, and I park under the

shade of a big blackjack oak then sit in the car feeling inadequate and guilty. Aunt Bonnie Kathleen molded me in the Jane Wyatt tradition and I sat around, mealymouthed, while Howard did the same thing to this daughter of mine.

And look how all that turned out—me running away, and Kate married to another Robert Young TV character, who is at this very moment on the golf green hitting little balls into holes while my daughter is in the kitchen. Barefoot and pregnant, but for the grace of modern contraception.

I know this because it's a Sunday afternoon ritual. The only thing that changes is the recipe. While Rick golfs, Kate gets out plastic bowls and a big wooden spoon so Bonnie can "cook" without fear of hurting herself.

I'm still in the car getting up my courage when my precocious granddaughter bursts through the front door with chocolate smears on her face, and Doggie, her favorite plush animal, squeezed under her arm.

"Nana's here, Nana's here!" Bonnie races down the sidewalk, leaps into my arms and covers my face with gooey kisses.

"That's some mighty sweet kisses, angel baby. Can I have about a million?"

How can I possibly leave? What in the world was

I thinking? Jenny has an independent streak a mile wide and doesn't need anybody and all Howard needs is three square meals and the evening news, but Bonnie needs me.

She giggles then wiggles down to race back into the kitchen where she jabs her fingers into the dough.

"Want some, Nana?" She holds a sticky finger out to me, and while I nibble the raw dough, Kate leans over and pecks me on the cheek.

"It's so good to see you, Mom."

"You, too."

I give her a reciprocal peck, feeling like a fraud. How did this happen? Was I too busy making sure Howard didn't turn Jenny into *Father Knows Best* and June Cleaver clones to bridge this gap between my older daughter and me?

"You want some coffee? I've made a fresh pot." Kate buys gourmet coffee—the kind you grind—and serves it in china cups with real cream.

"I could use a cup of good, stout Folgers."

Kate gives me a look. "It's Southern pecan, but I can run down to the store and get Folgers if that's what you want."

"For Pete's sake, Kate. Why don't you just tell me to shut up and drink what you've got?"

"What's gotten into you?"

"Nothing, and that's part of the trouble."

"Mother!"

Kate always calls me *Mother* when she disapproves of me, which is every Sunday, most holidays and any given weekday. Who can blame her? I failed her. Big-time.

Now would be a perfect time to clear the air, tell a few truths, but we Holt women have a long history of keeping silent. And when the air gets too rancid to breathe, we just start looking for a gas mask.

"Southern pecan is fine," I say, taking the easy way out.

"Good."

Kate pours a cup, and we both settle into a familiar pattern with relief. I hold on to the china cup while my daughter talks about the preschool she's selected for Bonnie to attend in the fall, the Christmas charity ball she's chairing this year, the new pool she and Rick are planning to build.

If I vanished off the face of the Earth in the next two minutes, Kate would still carry on in beautiful style.

Which is a very good thing. Still…being needed is lovely and comforting.

"Nana." Bonnie climbs into my lap. "Will 'ou sing wif me?"

"Certainly, sweet pea."

She launches into an exuberant, baby-voiced rendition of "Twinkle, Twinkle, Little Star," and while I sing along I wonder if she'll always be joyful or if she'll lose the spark, learn to settle, turn into Jane Wyatt.

A fierce courage overtakes me, and suddenly I know that whatever it takes, whatever I have to do, my granddaughter will always be able to say, *Nana never settled.*

"Kate...I'm..." *Leaving* sounds too harsh, too final. Impossible to explain over a cup of coffee. I don't even know whether it's the right word. Not really. "Going on an extended vacation."

"Without Dad?"

"He's too busy to get away." There I go again, beating around the bush. But in my defense, this is not a full-blown lie.

"Just what does an *extended* vacation mean, Mom?"

I should have known Kate would see right through me. Not only does she have Howard's big brown eyes that narrow at the first hint of suspicion, she also has his radarlike mind.

"You know how tired I've been from five years of going from one end of the state to the other to take care of Aunt Bonnie Kathleen."

"You didn't answer my question." She's staring at me through slits now. "Where are you going all of a sudden? Why couldn't you tell us about this last Wednesday night when we all went out for dinner?"

I breathe deeply, hoping to work up courage for a real soul-baring session, but all I get is a big whiff of Kate's magnolia-scented potpourri that makes me sneeze.

"You've been living with a trial lawyer too long."

I try for the light touch, but fail miserably, mainly because Bonnie is tilting her head, beaming her big smile at me.

"Can I go on bacation wif 'ou, Nana?"

I squeeze my coffee cup and blink hard. I should have taken the coward's way out; I should have said goodbye on the phone.

I squeeze her tight, then set her on the floor and grab my purse. "Not this time, sweet baby. See you later, alligator."

"Af'er while, c'ocodile."

"Mom?" Kate follows me to the door, tall and elegant, even in jeans, her dark hair pulled back in a ponytail. She could be a young Audrey Hepburn if she had a gamine's smile instead of Howard's serious look. "What in the world's going on?"

"I have to go, Kate. I'll call you."

I barrel through the door without looking back. Bonnie's calling, "Bye-bye," and I know her little hand is waving in the air. If I look back I'll turn to a pillar of salt. At the very least.

Maybe I will anyway. The tears that blind me and drip into the corners of my mouth taste salty. I'm a foolish old wreck. Fumbling with the car keys and a tissue at the same time, I'm finally able to drive down the street.

There was never a question about the direction I'll go. I turn south toward the Gulf, south toward the clean, hopeful expanse of sea. But not south toward the Mississippi Gulf Coast where I was born. I have too many relatives there, too many nosy cousins on Mother's side of the family who would wonder why I'd come, how long I was going to stay and why Howard was not with me.

Instead I head a bit eastward toward Alabama, aiming to travel back roads all the way to Pensacola, Florida. This destination feels right, partially, I think, because one of the last good memories of Howard is the vacation we took six years ago where we did nothing but read, eat great seafood and comb the beaches for sand dollars. Once, in a fit of wine-fueled ecstasy, we even made love in the afternoon. Something we hadn't done since the early days of our marriage. It was so unexpected that it's forever engraved in my mind.

By the time I get to Columbus, sixty miles down the road, I'm starving. Traveling always makes me hungry. I've never been on a road trip—nor an air trip, either—where I didn't pack a snack bag.

When I pull into Little Dooey's for barbecue, I wish I were driving something besides a Cadillac. Beside all the Jeep Wranglers and pickups and low-slung Mazdas with spinner hubcaps, my Cadillac looks like an old lady's car. I console myself by ordering an extralarge portion of pulled pork, but then realize that's exactly something dowdy, over-weight Elizabeth Martin would do.

I switch to a smaller order; Beth Holt Martin, a woman not only rediscovering herself but also trying to locate her hip bones.

After I eat I still have hours to go before sunset, but I'll be traveling sparsely populated countryside, so I consult my road maps to be certain I can make it to Demopolis, Alabama before dark. It's the only city on my route big enough to have a motel.

By the time I get there, Howard will be home. I

picture how he'll react when he sees my note on the kitchen table. He'll read it, then set his suitcase down and read it again in case he missed some nuance the first time around. Next he'll fold it into precise thirds, put it in his pocket and walk through the house to see what's missing. He'll check my closet and decide that whatever wild hare I'm chasing will soon wear itself out because every garment I own is still hanging there.

Then he'll order take-out Chinese and watch the evening news before he calls me on my cell phone. This methodical, steady behavior makes him the man you want to have around in a crisis. Unless it's a crisis of the heart, the spirit.

What I really want is for him to jerk up his phone and yell, "Elizabeth, come home! I can't live without you!"

Passion, that's what I want. Blazing comets and Fourth of July parades and Christmas lights all rolled into one. And not just passion in the bedroom... though certainly that's a huge chunk of it. I want to live fully, to embrace life with arms and heart and mind wide-open.

This is more than a road trip; it's a long journey to discover who I am and who I want to be.

By the time I cross the Black Warrior River into Demopolis, the sun is setting. Nothing is more spec-

tacular than sunset and sunrise reflected in water. If
I had thought to call ahead I might have been able to
rent a little cabin on the river where I could spend the
rest of the evening watching the drama of the heavens—sunset painting rainbows on the water followed
by a full moon and stars so bright they seem to explode
in the night sky.

Instead I take a room at the Holiday Inn and call
Howard rather than waiting for him to call me.

"Elizabeth, where the devil are you?"

"I'm okay, Howard, and I'd rather not say."

"Don't you think you could have at least discussed
this with me? My Lord, Elizabeth, you've run away
like some hormone-fueled teenager."

"I'm not running away, Howard. I'm an adult driving my own car."

He sighs, and I picture him sinking into his re-
cliner, running his hands over his receding hairline,
adjusting his glasses. Little things I used to find endearing. Now all they do is irritate me.

I wonder if this is merely a sign of creeping age,
this impatience. Maybe I don't need to run away.
Maybe I just need a pill. A great, big *be patient, this
too shall pass* pill.

Howard has never been at a loss for words, but the

silence stretches on so long I realize I've finally rendered him speechless. I feel a tug of compassion, a pinch of guilt, more than a little urge to say, "Don't worry, dear. Everything will be all right."

Lord, I'm a head case. Hot one minute, cold the next. Will she run or will she stay? Will she keep going or will she tuck her tail and go home?

Maybe I belong on one of those talk shows, such as *Dr. Phil*.

"Listen, Howard. I just need some time to sort out a few things."

"I thought that's what you were doing in Huntsville."

"Well, I didn't."

"Why can't you do your sorting at home?"

"I don't know. I just can't, that's all."

"That's just great, Elizabeth."

Of course, he doesn't mean great at all. What he means is *that's ridiculous*, and all of sudden I remember our honeymoon, the way he looked at me when I waltzed out of the bathroom in my new white lace gown and negligee, the way his eyes got hot and my hands got sweaty. Back then I thought Howard would always look at me that way, as if I were queen of his universe. I thought I'd always be stirred by the sight of his crooked smile, his square hands with the sprinkling of dark hair along the tops and the thumbs that curved backward. Why his thumbs moved me is a complete mystery. And why they no longer have any effect at all is equally mysterious.

It's my turn to sigh.

"Howard, the girls both know. They're fine with this."

"You discussed this with our daughters and didn't even bother to tell me?"

If voices were places, Howard's would be the tundra. Frostiness is not new to us, though. Usually at this point I wheedle and placate and he forgives me and we climb into the same bed where he pecks me on the cheek and then rolls over so no part of his body touches mine.

Thank God I don't have to lie on my side of the bed tonight, being careful not even to brush my feet against his while the rest of me burns with a lust that would be the envy of sixteen-year-olds. One of the ironies of life is that when men are in their prime, women don't know diddly-squat about intimacy, and when women enter their prime, men are either tapering off or searching for Viagra.

"Listen, Howard, I don't know when I'll be back."

I don't even know if I'll go back at all. That's one of the things I have to find out. "Don't try to find me. And call only in case of emergency."

"Define emergency, Elizabeth."

"For Pete's sake. You don't have to make a federal case out of this."

"What do you want me to do? Relax and enjoy it? Throw a party and celebrate?"

"You know what? That just pisses me off."

"That makes two of us."

"I'm not fixing to spend the evening quarreling with you."

"If this is about last night, Elizabeth, I told you I was just too tired. I'm not a performing seal, you know."

"You're always too tired, Howard."

His hot silence blisters my eardrums. I can almost see his bald spot turning red. Which is exactly one of the reasons I never tell him anything. Confrontation leads to all sorts of unladylike behavior, and I'm a girl—past my prime, granted, but we won't get into that—who was taught to mind her manners.

"Is that what this is about, Elizabeth? Sex?"

"I didn't say that."

"No, you didn't say anything. You never do."

Now it's my turn to curl what's left of his hair with a weighty silence. My stomach's churning, and I'd blame it on my barbecue dinner if I didn't know better. It's all that unsaid stuff knocking around, looking for a way out.

Maybe I'll put it in a letter.

Someday.

"You don't give me a chance, Howard. You know every damned thing."

"You don't have to use that kind of language, Elizabeth."

"If I'd wanted a lecture I'd have dialed 1-800-God and asked to talk to Aunt Bonnie Kathleen."

I don't give him a chance to say anything else before hanging up. Instead I climb into my Cadillac and drive to the marina where I stomp around until my anger wears off. Then I settle into a quiet stroll, enjoying the path of moonlight on the water and the mournful sound of an oncoming barge.

I wonder where it's going.

I wonder where I'm going. Not my short-term destination, but my lifelong one. Somewhere wonderful, I hope.

CHAPTER 3

"If I break my fool neck, who'll find me
in an empty house?"
—Howard

All my life I've viewed myself as a reasonable man, so when I found Elizabeth's note I didn't overreact: I folded it and stuck it in my pocket thinking it was another of her jokes. Not that she's played one on me in a long time, but she used to be quite a prankster.

Take, for instance, that Halloween when Kate was a freshman at the "W" and Jenny was staying overnight with friends… Elizabeth loves all holidays, especially Halloween, so there we sat in our matching recliners reading, a tray of popcorn balls and candied apples towering between us.

Elizabeth turned down the page in her book and said, "You might as well take off the Frankenstein outfit. I don't think anybody is coming."

She'd gone to a lot of trouble to buy the costume and do my monster makeup, and I couldn't bear the thought of her being disappointed. "Just wait and see, Elizabeth. Somebody will show up."

"You wait, Howard. I'm going to take a bath."

When I heard the water running upstairs I thought about calling the new young couple across the street and asking them to bring their children over, but I decided to wait it out. Surely somebody would show.

The doorbell rang just as I was settling back into my novel. Al Young's *Seduction by Light*. I remember it well. He's now the poet laureate of California. Anyway, I called Elizabeth to tell her we had trick-or-treaters, but she didn't answer—probably still in the tub—so I picked up the tray and hurried to the door.

There stood this woman with her back to me, wearing a red fright wig, black trench coat and flip-flops. Not much of a costume, if you asked me. Still, if adults wanted to go parading around the neighborhood dressed like that, who was I to judge?

I cleared my throat and all of a sudden she whirled around and flung her coat open, naked as a jaybird. I'm talking not a stitch.

"Trick or treat," she yelled, and all I could see was this long expanse of advancing flesh, pale as a new moon. Naturally I moved back, but I miscalculated the location of the umbrella stand, crashed sideways and gashed my head.

The way Elizabeth tells it, I screamed and leaped back, but of course she'd say that because her version makes everybody laugh harder, and she does love to do her public comic routines. Or used to.

Anyhow, I had to have stitches. She wanted to rush me right to the emergency room, but I told her I was not going to die within the next five minutes and besides, the doctors would take us more seriously if I ditched the Frankenstein look and she ditched the fright wig and put on some underwear.

So you can see why I treated her note as some kind of joke. After I checked her closet and discovered she'd taken nothing with her, I was even more convinced that she was either playing a prank or suffering from some temporary fit of anger that would wear itself out by the time she got to the mall or wherever she was going.

When I saw that she hadn't cooked dinner and that Rufus was slinking around as though he'd lost his best friend, I deduced that she wasn't joking, she was mad, so I just ordered Chinese takeout for one—no use subsidizing her bad behavior—and settled in to watch the evening news. I'd give her time to cool off, then I'd call her cell phone and politely inquire what was going on.

You can imagine my surprise when she called me and announced out of the blue that she had run away from home.

It's hard to shake my cool. That's why I'm so successful in my profession. My patients confide secrets that would make an ordinary person lose sleep at night, but I'm renowned for my ability to never internalize their problems. I'm that way at home, too. Living with a houseful of women, that's a darned good thing. All those raging hormones. All the angst and drama and tears.

But Elizabeth's phone call shook me. That's why it took a while for the truth to sink in: my wife has left me.

So now here I am in the unnerving quiet of an empty house with nothing to keep me company except a box of congealing Chinese food and a depressed dog.

I'm a logical man; if I think about something long enough I can always decipher a problem, find a solution. But no matter how many ways I wrap my mind around Elizabeth's sudden departure, I can't come up with any answers.

Why did my wife run away? I thought she was happy. Sure, we've had our ups and downs just like any ordinary couple, but I can't think of a single incident that would make her want to leave.

Granted, I'm no longer Tarzan in the bedroom, but she said she didn't leave me because of sex, and I believe her. Elizabeth's not a shallow person.

But what if it's not me? What if it's somebody else?

My wife with another man. The thought chills me to the bone.

Elizabeth and I swore we'd never sneak around, especially after Jeff Jones from down the street hightailed it with Wanda Slocoam, as well as the diamond bracelet he'd bought for his wife, Laura, for Christmas.

I can still see Elizabeth standing in her bathrobe with her hands on her hips after she heard the news.

"If you find somebody else, you just come right out and tell me, Howard."

"I'd never do such a thing, Elizabeth," I told her.

"If you do, she'd better be older than my tennis shoes. If she's not I'll come flog you with my full-support bra."

I thought we had this sort of unspoken pact of fidelity and honesty, but what if she's found somebody younger and more virile, somebody with all his hair? Of course, he'd have only half my brains, but still...

I go into the bathroom and look in the mirror to see if I can see myself as Elizabeth does.

Good God! My hair—or what's left of it—looks like that limp stuff you throw into the street during parades and then everybody comes along and stomps on it. I try to hide the balding spot by combing a few strands over it, but it's not quite long enough. Maybe if I let it grow a bit…

Loss and a sense of failure squeeze my chest so hard I slump against the sink.

What did I do to deserve this? Nothing, that's what. I've provided everything a good husband should, and more. Our house is one of the most expensive in the neighborhood, I buy flowers and jewelry with real stones on her birthday, and I trade in our cars every year. One for me, one for her. If she'd wanted a Mercedes instead of a Cadillac, why didn't she tell me? Heck, I'd get her a Jaguar if that's what it takes to make her happy.

She doesn't even have to work. I make more than enough to support my family. Have from the day I hung out my shingle.

After we married, Elizabeth was band director at Milam Middle School, but I could see how hard it was for her when Kate came along, juggling babysitters and band concerts. So when Jenny was born, I said, "Just quit that job and stay home, hon. Concentrate on the kids and that symphony you've always wanted to write."

What does it take to make a woman a happy? And how are you supposed to know what they want if they don't tell you?

I'm a psychiatrist, for Pete's sake. It's my job to get people to open up and express their feelings. How could I have failed with my own wife?

It feels as if there's a gaping hole beside me, a huge airless space where Elizabeth ought to be. I actually think I might be having a heart attack. It would serve her right.

Instantly I regret the thought. I'm not petty and vindictive. I don't cuss, I don't smoke, I don't run around and I don't drink. Well, social drinking and maybe an occasional nightcap, but that's all. I'm a good provider, a good father, a good husband. At least I thought I was. Until today.

My legs feel as if they're buckling, so I sink onto the toilet seat. Who would pick me up if I fell down and broke my fool neck?

When the phone rings, I jump like somebody shot. *Elizabeth.* Calling again to say she's sorry, she's out of her mind, she doesn't know what possessed her, she's coming home immediately.

Of course, I'll tell her to wait until morning. No use taking chances on a dark road. *See*. That's the kind of husband I am. Thoughtful. Considerate.

In my haste to get to the phone I nearly trip on the rug.

"Daddy? You sound out of breath." It's Kate. "Are you okay?"

"I'm fine."

I clear my throat around this lie. But, by George, I've never showed weakness around my children, and I'm not fixing to start now. A child needs to look up to her father.

"How are you, hon?"

"I don't know. I'm worried about Mom."

"What did your mother tell you?"

"Oh Lord, Daddy...nothing. A big fat zero. Just that she was going on a mysterious, extended vacation."

"How did she look? How did she sound?"

"Normal, I guess. But then, Mom's let herself go recently, so maybe something's going on that we don't know about."

"You mean like cancer?"

Dogs go off to die. Maybe some women are like that. A phenomenon not covered in current psychology textbooks.

"Has she been to the doctor recently, Daddy?"

"No, she hasn't."

Elizabeth always tells me about her doctors' appointments. But then, she didn't even have the courtesy to tell me she was leaving home, so why wouldn't she keep a little thing like a doctor's appointment secret?

"Are you saying you think your mother's sick?"

"I don't know. Maybe. She's gained all that weight. Of course, you'd know if she had a psychological problem."

"Of course." I can't bear to admit the truth, can't bear to be a failure in the eyes of my daughter, too.

I hear my own sigh echoed in my daughter, then we both just hold on to the phone, not saying anything. Finally she says, "Daddy, I don't quite know how to handle this. Mother's always been right there at home."

"I know."

This house is not even a home without her. She has this knack… I don't know how she does it, but she can turn even the cheapest motel room into a place that makes you want to settle down, take off your shoes and dream awhile.

"I keep wondering if it's something I've said. I can be pretty blunt and Mother's sensitive."

"Of course not, Kate. You put that out of your head. Mom will be back home before you can say, 'Jack Robinson.'"

That's what I used to tell the children when Elizabeth had to go out of town with the band. It always helped.

I wish reassurance were that simple now.

"Of course you're right, Daddy. She said it was just a little vacation. Is there anything I can do to help you while she's gone?"

"I don't want to be any trouble."

"You're no trouble. Besides, Rick's working on that big hospital lawsuit and Bonnie and I have all kinds of time. Just tell me what you need, and I'll take care of it."

"It would be nice to come home to something besides takeout for dinner."

"Oh, that's no problem. I'll just cook early and bring over a plate to leave in the warmer till you get home."

"Thank you, hon. And if it's not too much bother, could you see that my white shirts get to the laundry? I've got that jury consulting job in Nashville on Wednesday, and I don't want to end up without any clean shirts."

"You leave it to me, Daddy."

I don't know what I would do without Kate. Of

course, I have Jenny, too, but I'd expect snow in August before she'd call to check on me. Not that Jenny and I have any major problems, but she's always been closer to Elizabeth.

Of course, judging by the way I've floundered around my wife's emotional terrain, I could be free-falling from an airplane with Jenny and never know I didn't even have a parachute.

Jenny's more complicated than Kate, more like her mother. Both of them have a wild kind of energy that reminds me of a tornado brewing.

Elizabeth thinks our youngest is going through a typical breaking-free phase, but that's not true. Jenny's always been restless and willful. And her recent actions are just plain irresponsible, even if she has been friends with the Clark boys and Sara London since first grade. If Elizabeth had sided with me, we could have stopped this backpacking trip out west, and Jenny wouldn't be traipsing off God-knows-where doing God-knows-what right now. They're probably going to places like Hooters.

Who knows if she even has a cell phone signal? I could have a stroke and die and it might take six weeks to locate her.

I'm going to tell Kate that if I die she can just go

ahead and have the funeral without Jenny. Elizabeth, too, by George.

These thoughts are unworthy of me, but sometimes self-righteous indignation is the only thing that feels good.

Up until today life was simple. I had a home, a wife and kids, respect. All of a sudden I'm a psychiatrist with a dark side, a churlish, failed husband who wishes insomnia, warts and bad breath on everybody who has hurt him.

Especially if that Somebody is off with another man. I might as well face the facts: Elizabeth still has this sort of magnetic appeal, but nobody would describe me as appealing. I look more like Barry Goldwater than Tom Cruise…and Goldwater's been dead for years.

My feet feel heavy going up the stairs. I might as well take an aspirin now or I won't sleep a wink. Good Lord, while my wife's off skylarking, I have to deal with patients threatening to kill themselves.

I shake two aspirin out of the bottle. Extrastrength. If it gives me heart palpitations, that's all her fault.

I brush my teeth, put on my pajamas, then go into the bedroom and just stare at the bedcovers. Elizabeth always turns back the bed. Not that I can't. But that one simple gesture is a small way for my wife to show she appreciates my hard work, she appreciates the freedom she has to stay home all day and do exactly as she pleases.

I turn back my side, crawl in and turn off the bedside lamp. It's only after I've pulled up the sheet and folded it under my chin that I remember I didn't floss my teeth. I didn't even put on clean pajamas. This will be three days for the blue-striped pair.

I'm not fixing to get up and do it after I've finally settled in. For one thing, the aspirin is beginning to take effect, and I might fall down and hurt myself.

For another, I don't want to see Elizabeth's side of the bed. Empty.

CHAPTER 4

"When did sand in your swimsuit stop
being sexy?"

—Beth

Last night's phone call from Howard tightened me up like a piano wire. I feel as if I've been driving three weeks instead of only three hours from Demopolis to Pensacola. When I get out of the car, I have to do stretches to unkink myself.

I don't know what possesses me to stay at the same motel Howard and I stayed when we came to the Florida panhandle six years ago. The Palm Breeze. It's the closest thing we could find to the little mom-and-pop motel where we spent our honeymoon, the kind that used to dot the Gulf Coast before it became homogenized in the name of progress. Pink stucco, a concrete patio out back featuring wind chimes, molded plastic chairs and pink plastic flamingoes.

Anyway…here I am, checking in without a suit-case. Standing in a lobby not much bigger than my walk-in closet with my slacks sweat-stuck to the back of my legs, my hair wilted and the elastic of my panties bunched up and pinching my waist.

The young man behind the counter looks like the Incredible Hulk, except deeply tanned instead of green. He's hunched in a straight-backed chair immersed in a Spider-Man comic book, oblivious to a potential customer.

"I want a room with a view," I tell him.

Finally he looks up. "What view are you talking about?"

"That lovely little park at the back, you know, the one with the live oak trees and the Spanish moss hanging down and that charming little wooden carousel."

"The only view you're going to get is the new Wal-Mart they put in over the park last year."

I've never heard so-called progress described exactly that way. *Put in.*

A shaded playground for children vanished, hundred-year-old trees destroyed, an oasis of tranquility and beauty raped. Why didn't somebody protest? Why didn't the neighborhood's parents carry signs and petition the city council and contact the newspaper?

"Lady." The hulking young man—Larry, his name tag reads—shifts a wad of something from his left jaw to his right. Chewing gum? Tobacco? "Do you want a room or not?"

"I do."

My feet are swollen, my legs are aching and I need to pee. The trip took a bigger toll than I expected.

I hand over my credit card. A woman with enough money to pay in full when the bill comes. But, of course, it will be sent to Tupelo, and I'll be in Pensacola.

Or will I? The thought of not knowing where I'll be a week, two weeks, two months from now is unsettling and exhilarating at the same time. Like being a teenager and not knowing what you want to do the rest of your life or where you want to live or who you want to live with. The future full of mystery and promise.

For an instant I have a crazy desire to call Howard and say, "Listen, you ought to come down and join me. We could start over, not in a plodding, methodical, making-plans sort of way, but wild and free, our lives unfurling like a kite that just broke free and lifted toward the sun."

Instead I go into room 126, head straight to the bathroom and pull open the blinds to stare at Wal-Mart. At least my view is of the garden center. A bank of red hibiscus sits near the curb. No mistaking the huge, crepe-paper-like blossoms. And yellow allamanda. Another easy-to-spot tropical. Pots and pots of multihued impatiens. A rack of ferns, wilting in the sun.

Today is the day I always water my Boston ferns. I wonder if Howard will remember. They're picky. They want daily misting and regular feeding. Otherwise the leaves will curl under and turn brown.

I grab the cell phone from my purse and punch in numbers.

"Hello," Howard says. "Hello?"

I can't have it both ways. I can't live two lives, the old one in Mississippi and the new one in Florida. New. Exciting. Scary.

"Elizabeth? Say something."

I punch End, and the act seems fraught with weighty significance.

My phone begins to ring, but when Howard's number flashes on the screen, I don't answer. What would I say? He's going to ask questions and I don't have any answers.

Finally the ringing stops. It's one in the afternoon and I haven't had lunch. But who cares? I'm no longer bound by the clock. I can eat breakfast at eleven and lunch at four if I want. Or no breakfast, no lunch, no dinner. I can just eat ice cream all day, whenever I get hungry.

But I haven't kicked the living-by-the-clock habit yet, and as I stare at my watch the rest of the day stretches before me, hours of time that are mine to fill as I please. I can drive to the beach, lie in the sun, buy binoculars and scan the horizon for bottlenose dolphins. Or I can browse the bookstores, select a sackful of books and do nothing but read and eat potato chips without having to worry about getting dinner on time.

Once I read a book about a woman going through menopause who stopped making dinner. Just stopped. While her family asked, "What's for dinner?" she sat on the front porch swing and stared at a gardenia bush. Although white flies were sucking the life out of it and it was her prize bush, she didn't even get up to spray it with neem oil.

Of course, I'm not like that fictional character. My flight has nothing to do with the change of life and everything to do with the quality of life.

But where do I start? My choices are mind-boggling. On the one hand I want to drift along, meander through my days without agenda or destination, and on the other I feel the urge to make some kind of long-range plan.

First, though, I settle in, unpack my toothbrush in the fifties-style bathroom—wall-hung lavatory with the plumbing showing, uneven pink tile floor, pink toilet—then stow my underwear in the top dresser drawer and my unfinished symphony in the bedside table.

There are no frills in this room. No notepads and pens stamped with the motel's name. No desk. No matching bedspread and draperies. A pink chenille spread covers the bed and yellowing Venetian blinds cover the window.

This unstylish room is a throwback to a time when life was simpler, kinder, slower-paced. It's the kind of room where I can cocoon myself—rest, heal, grow.

The first step is to get to the seaside where I once dreamed. When I was eight I saw an entire pod of dolphins cavorting in the Mississippi Sound and imagined myself becoming a marine biologist, a fearless woman who communed with these gentle giants to unlock the mysteries of the sea. At twelve I heard the symphony of the ocean and fell in love with music forever. At twenty-two I stood at the water's edge and exchanged vows with Howard, believing the touch of his hand would always be magic.

The dreams changed with age, but not the source. It was always the ebb and flow of tides that brought them to the surface.

I head to Wal-Mart, then sprint through the aisles selecting a beach towel, sunscreen, toiletries, a couple of romance novels, T-shirts, shorts, nightshirts and a skirted swimsuit that looks like something Mamie Eisenhower would wear. I'm headed to the checkout counter when I dash back down the housewares aisle. Every woman making herself over needs twelve gardenia candles in cranberry-colored glass votive cups.

After a whirlwind trip back to the Palm Breeze to change clothes and grab my unfinished symphony, I'm on my way to the beach.

It's still a little early for the summer crowd, so I have the beach to myself except for a young mother sounding frazzled as she tells her three little boys not to go out too deep and a handsome gray-haired couple with faces as tanned and wrinkled as peach pits sitting side by side in lawn chairs, holding hands.

That's how I imagined it would be with Howard and me. I feel as if I ought to walk over there and congratulate them, ask them, *How did you keep romance alive?* Instead I leave my belongings on my towel and race toward the water. Well, waddle, is more like it, but in my mind I'm svelte and sixteen, as light and carefree as dandelions in the wind.

A strong swimmer, I enjoy the feel of gliding through the water watching the shore recede. Though there are always shark sightings along these beaches and incidents of shark attacks, there are no fishing boats, which lessens the likelihood of seeing these fierce predators. They come in for bait, especially in early morning and late afternoon.

I float with my face to the sun while seagulls soar overhead and a brown pelican dives for fish. Buoyed by salty water I lie perfectly still, listening to the music of life teeming around me, and then I head back to shore.

Sand squishes between my wet toes and sprinkles across my towel like sugar, but that's part of the beach experience. When Howard and I were courting in Ocean Springs, we used to lie on a beach towel kissing and laughing about the taste and feel of grit between us.

Now I just squirm around trying to get comfortable. Sand has sifted everywhere, including the crotch of my swimsuit, and I discover there's nothing sexy about it when nobody's there to appreciate it.

This is the age of loss—kids striking out on their own, people dying, husbands turning indifferent, wives flying the coop. And yet...the senior couple is now strolling on the beach, arms around each other's waists, hips and thighs touching. Birdlike, the wife tilts her face upward, and her tall husband leans down to kiss her.

Envy rears its ugly head, and hard on its heels a sense of failure. How did I let my marriage go so wrong?

Too much introspection is bad for the digestion.

I take my unfinished symphony out of my beach bag and try to put music on paper. Does this section need to be adagio sostenuto or allegretto? Do I need Beethoven's haunting melodies or Grieg's huge, crashing chords?

And where's Beth in all this?

The sweet older couple strolls past my blanket and I wave. Oh Lord. No wonder I can't write music. Until I figure out how Howard and I turned into *Who's Afraid of Virginia Woolf* instead of these beautiful geriatric lovers, I'm as blocked as somebody in need of a large dose of Kaopectate.

Instead of music, I put words in the treble clef.

Dear Howard,
I've lost my way and I can't tell you exactly why.

There was no one moment between us when I said, *This is it. I just can't take it anymore*. Instead I feel as if I've been standing out in a steady rain for a very long time, and I'm only just now realizing that I'm wet and cold.

The words pour out, presto agitato, rushing out on a wave of long bottled-up emotion. If I stop to think about what I'm doing I'll quit, because admitting this kind of fearsome truth makes me feel as though I'm standing in the middle of the street naked, my cottage-cheese thighs, gray pubic hair and all on display.

I had dreams once, Howard, big dreams. Of course you and the children are part of them, but nobody needs me that much anymore, except maybe Bonnie, and I'm left with this big gaping hole that somehow never got filled.

Out of the corner of my eye I watch the beautiful senior couple fold their blanket and steal away, hands linked and faces tilted toward each other, smiling. I can't remember the last time Howard and I smiled at each other like that. I can't remember the last time he came home and told me something funny that happened at the office, or I stood waiting at the door, bursting with news I wanted to share with him.

I continue writing, moving into the bass clef.

I'm not blaming you, Howard. I'm not blaming anybody, not really, not even Aunt Bonnie Kathleen, though she certainly knew how to hold a prancing filly on a tight rein.

I don't want to be the kind of woman I am anymore, the kind everybody consults only when they want to know the best way to remove rust stains from the toilet and dog stains from the rug. I don't want to be the kind of woman who worries about holding her stomach in and whose major decisions of the day are whether to buy rising flour or plain and what to cook for supper. I don't want the most important thing I do all day to be making sure the toilet paper rolls out because that's the way you like it.

I don't want to give a flying fart about crow's-feet and age spots and conventional opinions and dust bunnies under the sofa. I want to dance in the sunrise and race barefoot in the dew and roll naked between clean, crisp sheets feeling that every ounce of me, including my whale belly, is wonderful.

I chew my fingernails. Do I sound like a woman whose mind has flown the coop? Should I cross out the part about dreams? Will he think I'm blaming him because I never finished my symphony?

A breeze freshens over the bay, ruffles my hair and lifts it off my neck, catches my fear and blows it into small, manageable parts.

Howard, writing this letter feels like putting on my most comfortable sweatpants and not caring that the waistband is stretched and the holes show. I always wondered what it would be like to visit you professionally, lie on the couch and tell you my thoughts, and I guess that's what I just did.

I don't know whether I can mail this letter, but writing it feels like opening a cage door and letting loose a cat that has been trapped inside, clawing me to pieces.

Back in my motel room, I tuck the letter into the top drawer of the bedside table, circle the room trying to decide what to do next. I feel like a dime-store Santa after Christmas. No more people lined up clamoring for my attention.

Not cooking supper, not having Kate pop by with Bonnie, not having Jenny bouncing downstairs on her way to the movies feels strange. I pick up the phone to call both girls, but all I get is *Hi, leave a message at the beep.*

All of sudden I don't even know what kind of message to leave. I can no longer say, *I've made apple pie, come over for dinner.* The beep sounded long ago, and I feel foolish just hanging up. Finally I say, "Hi, it's me, give me a call," stilted and formal, as if my family has already disappeared from my life.

I can't stand this intense loneliness another minute. When I arrive in the lobby, out of breath, Larry looks up from a science textbook, of all things.

"Ms. Martin, isn't it?"

"Yes. Just call me Beth."

Human contact. I feel rescued.

"You seem in an awful hurry. Is anything wrong?"

"Nothing that can't be helped by a friendly smile and some comfort food. Preferably chocolate."

"This is your lucky day."

Larry gives me a big, cheerful smile and a handful

of chocolate-covered mints from the bowl sitting on the check-in desk. Then he leans against the front of the desk, still smiling.

"How's that?"

"Much better."

I eat two candies, settle into the lobby's only chair and ask Larry about himself. He's a student at Pensacola Junior College and has a cute girlfriend named Tammy. I show him pictures of my family.

This is the lovely thing about giving more than a passing hello to the people we encounter: each time we reach out to another human being we are blessed. Today my blessing is in not feeling alone.

Day two I wake up expecting to feel different, transformed somehow, a woman unfurling her wings. But the only thing different about me is my sassy new nightshirt, which reads Well-Behaved Women Rarely Make History.

Nobody would call me well behaved anymore, so maybe I'm fixing to burst into artistic fame, a Mississippi musical version of Grandma Moses.

To celebrate I place my twelve scented candles around the tub, pour in bubble bath and lean back to luxuriate. My decadent pleasure lasts all of two minutes and then I'm floundering around trying to get my head under water. Instead of bursting into fame, I've burst into flame: I leaned too close the candles and my hair caught fire.

Fortunately, it was on the back and just a tiny spot, so nobody notices, not Larry, who is at the desk again, nor the sweet old couple who wave when I spread my blanket on the beach.

I smile and wave back, and then pick up my cell phone to check on my daughters, Jenny first because our relationship is free of the guilt I feel over Kate.

"Hi, Jen girl. How's it going?"

"Mom! I'm great, fantastic." Jenny recounts her tours of red canyons and swirling vortexes, and then we laugh about the bubble bath and the candles.

Afterward, I sit on my blanket watching the older couple wade into the water, holding hands. I fall into the moment—the beauty of their love, the sunshine on my back, the smell of the sea—and let myself drift there until I've found a peaceful center, a place of serenity and succor.

Then I pick up the phone to call Kate.

CHAPTER 5

"How do you get rid of tarnish on a hero?"
—Kate

I thought my mother was perfect until she took off to parts unknown without a minute's notice. She entertains with the pizzazz of Martha Stewart, can talk to anybody with the ease and wit of Oprah and collects friends just by walking into a room. Daddy and Jenny and Bonnie adore her and I idolize her.

Or did until she ran away, and now I don't know what to think. Has she been unhappy all these years and merely covering it up or is something happening to her that is too awful to tell?

If I didn't have Bonnie and Rick, I guess I'd be going plumb crazy instead of only halfway. As it is, I nearly jump out of my skin when the phone rings and Mom's number pops up. Ordinarily I'd be eager to talk, but now I think about letting it ring because I don't know how much more of this drama I can handle.

That's why I didn't call her back last night. What do you say to a mother who has always been your hero and suddenly she's acting like somebody you hardly know?

My voice mail is fixing to kick in, and at the last minute I pick up the phone and say hello.

"Kate, thank goodness."

What does that mean? *Thank goodness?* Is she fixing to tell me she needs a kidney transplant and has run off because the doctors can't find a kidney and she can't stand to die in front of her family—which is ridiculous because she's never had a single kidney problem.

See how upset this whole thing has made me? I'm no longer rational. Last night I put salt into the cake instead of sugar and had to throw the whole thing into the garbage disposal and start all over.

"How are you? How're Bonnie and Rick?"

"Bonnie's jumping up and down with excitement about play school. And Rick's working too hard, as usual."

The only thing I can say about myself is that I'm confused, and so I don't say anything.

"How's Rufus?"

The dog? She's asking about the dog and not Daddy? How bizarre is that.

"He's not his usual perky self, but then neither is Daddy. When are you coming home?"

"Oh… I don't know. Certainly not by Wednesday. I've got to call Emmaline and tell her I won't be at her book club luncheon."

I could care less about Emmaline's society luncheons, contrary to what my husband wants me to think. If it were left up to him I'd be a member of every women's club in Tupelo for the express purpose of bandying his name about as Tupelo's answer to Perry Mason.

"Are you visiting friends, vacationing alone, what?"

"I'm just trying to sort things out."

"What things? Have we done something to upset you? Have I?"

"Oh, for goodness sake. No. You're a good daughter and…"

It's that long pause that gets to me. All my life I've tried to measure up, but I've been a day late and a dollar short, as Aunt Bonnie Kathleen used to say. Not that Mom has ever said anything to indicate that I've failed her, but I've always known that I was second best. It showed in the way her face lit up when Jenny entered a room, in their easy laughter, in the way the two of them stood united while Dad and I stood on the fringes—the only two in the room who didn't get the joke.

"...this simply has nothing to do with you, Kate."

"Are you and Dad having problems I don't know about?"

"No...and yes. Listen, Kate, a husband and wife will always have problems if they live together long enough. You let little things go by until suddenly they're like a pink elephant on your piano stool. You've got to either do something about it or hold your nose and pretend you don't smell the stench."

See, this is another thing I'm talking about. Jenny would laugh over the pink elephant reference, but I'm standing in my kitchen wondering why Mom won't come right out and tell me in plain English.

Not that I'm jealous of Jenny. It's just that I feel I've failed in some way to be the kind of person that would make Mom pat the covers on her bed (as she did with Jenny) and say, *Hop in and we'll giggle over secrets.*

"I know this all seems sudden and bizarre to you, Kate. You're rational like Howard."

See, that's just what I mean. Mom always views me as outside the exclusive girls' circle.

"Well…yeah, it does, Mom. I can't understand why you're not here working things out."

"I guess this sounds lame, but I have to work things out in my own way. And not just with your father. With me, Kate. I don't know who I am anymore, and until I do, I'm not of much use in Tupelo making pies on Sunday and doing the laundry on Tuesday."

Mom says goodbye, tells me she'll call again, and I go into the laundry room to take Rick's shirts out of the dryer feeling totally inadequate. What's wrong with doing laundry and making pies and keeping a nice house for your family? Mom did it for years without complaint. Am I going to wake up one day when I'm fifty and think, *Hey, I don't want to do this anymore?*

And why can't I talk to Mom about these things? Would she and I be laughing together and sharing confidences if I had run off like Jenny on the back of a Harley?

All of a sudden I can't bear to fold shirts. I go upstairs where Bonnie is sleeping and stand in her doorway thinking, *Please. Please don't ever let her feel as if she can't talk to her own mother.*

CHAPTER 6

"Is sleeping late a character flaw?"
—Beth

Day three: I decide that if I'm going to find myself, I might as well start with my cheekbones. Dressed in sweats over my swimsuit, I head to Pensacola Bay.

One of my best memories of growing up is jogging on the beach every morning with Aunt Bonnie Kathleen. While we did our warm-ups and cooldowns we'd talk, some of the few times we ever said anything more significant than *What time will you be home? What do you want for supper?* and *When was the last time you watered the petunias?*

I remember asking her one morning what she would do differently if she could start over.

"I'd wear real silk instead of the imitation kind," she said. "I'd get a manicure every week and I might even get a pedicure, too, and paint my toenails red."

At seventeen I didn't understand what Aunt Bonnie Kathleen, in her obscure way, was trying to tell me. At fifty-three I know she was saying she'd allow the real woman trapped inside to come out and face the world.

She never did allow that woman to come out, but thirty-six years later I'm bursting forth, shucking my cocoon and hoping to emerge the woman I was born to be. I don't know yet exactly who that is, but at the very least it's going to be a woman who is physically fit.

I park under the shade of a live oak, then walk briskly to the edge of the water to start my stretches, a few toe touches, which ought to be simple. The TV exercise gurus make this look easy, but believe me, they're lying. When I bend over, some body part I didn't know I had creaks, and for a minute I think I'm going to be stuck in this position for the rest of my life.

Grunting and groaning helps me get upright, and I decide to forego the warm-up. Just cut to the chase. Get on the sand and jog.

The first five yards are easy, but then things get complicated. Instead of spraying up behind my flying feet, the sand just sucks me in and tries to hold me captive.

A quarter mile down the beach I'm heaving and panting, convinced I'm fixing to die of exertion.

"Hello, there."

I look up to see the lovely elderly couple who frequent this beach, strolling from the opposite direction. Both tall and slender, they walk with the grace of dancers. I imagine this is how Ginger Rogers and Fred Astaire looked in their golden years. They introduce themselves as Ken and Irma Price, and then ask if there's anything they can do to help me.

"Oxygen and a wheelchair would be nice." When I laugh to show I'm kidding, they join in, and I hold out my hand. "Hi, I'm Beth Martin."

"We've been noticing you," Irma says. "You're new here, aren't you?"

"Yes. I'm from Tupelo."

"Welcome to Pensacola," Ken tells me, and when I thank him, he and his gracious wife continue their stroll.

I find the nearest sand dune to sit and catch my breath, then pull my cell phone out of my pocket to call Jane and tell her about my failed attempt to lose ten pounds.

"Lord, Beth, you can't do it all in one day."

"I won't do it at all if it involves this kind of exertion. I'm with Joan Rivers—if God had meant for me to bend over he'd have put diamonds on the floor."

"You didn't call just to tell me this, Beth."

"No, I called to ask about Howard. Have you seen or heard from him?"

"I saw him yesterday morning when he got the mail. We waved, but that's all."

"How did he look?"

"He was on his porch, I was on mine. Beth, if you're asking how he feels about your being gone, why don't you ask him? Or better yet, tell him how you feel."

"I wrote him a letter, but I didn't mail it."

"Why not?"

"I honestly don't know. Howard's always so *right*, and I'm always so…oh, I don't know…like somebody with two left feet. But, hey, what about you? What's going on?"

She tells me about her daughter-in-law Mary's promotion at the bank and her grandson Ben's new tooth. After we say goodbye I call Laura Phelps to take a rain check on our shopping trip to Memphis and Emmaline Brooks to cancel the book club luncheon.

I'm getting ready to call Grace York to tell her I won't be at the symphony board meeting when she calls me.

"Beth? I'm so glad I caught you. I've been trying to reach you at home, and finally got Howard. He gave me your cell phone number."

Isn't that just like Howard? He makes himself available to the whole world via his cell and can't understand why I only give my cell number to my family and my real friends. Grace is not one of them. She's chairman of the board I'm on, but other than that she just wants to pester me to death about meetings or drag some gossip out of me.

"I won't be at the board meeting Thursday night," I tell her.

"Yes, I heard that already. I never dreamed you and Howard were having trouble."

"I'm just vacationing, Grace."

"By yourself? I'd be careful about that if I were you. I know at least three women who'd be more than happy to snatch Howard up."

I don't ask Grace who, instead I tell her I have something important to take care of, and the minute I hang up I fall victim to small-town gossip. Who are those women and what will I do if Howard gets tired of waiting for a wife who ran away and decides to turn his attention—and his pocketbook—to somebody who's willing to stay home and wash his socks and give him the adoring Nancy Reagan smile?

Maybe I want him to, anyway. Maybe I don't want a future with Howard. But if that turns out to be true, I'd better darned well be prepared to fend for myself.

True, Aunt Bonnie Kathleen left me financially secure, but that money wouldn't be enough to last the rest of my life. If I'm truly going to be an independent woman—married or unmarried—I'd better figure out if I have what it takes to make my own living.

A svelte body will have to wait. Hurrying back to the Palm Breeze, I grab my composition book and sun hat, then sit on a pink plastic chair on the concrete patio and work on my symphony.

Day four: I am still at the Palm Breeze, a bit thinner, a bit more content and working on my symphony. But the only things I'm certain about are that I miss my children and friends, I miss my dog and truth to tell, I even miss Howard.

If I'm going to reinvent myself, I'd better get busy because so far I've only done about a tenth of the job. I could lie here all morning mulling over my future. Instead I roll out of bed at the crack of nine.

Thank goodness I'm not interested in getting

worms because I'm surely not an early bird. By the time I get to the beach and spread my gear, Ken and Irma are already there.

I wave and they wave, and then I wonder if my laggard ways explain why it has taken me twenty years to finish my symphony. If I had rolled out of bed at five instead of crawling back under the covers saying, *Oh God, it can't be morning,* maybe I'd have something to show for my time besides a stomach that looks like a cream-filled doughnut and untoned legs that scream, *Help!* after a quarter mile plod on the beach.

As much as I want to, I'm not going to call my children today because every time I do I'm sucked backward and end up feeling as if I've consigned them to orphanhood. Especially Kate.

I don't know what I'm going to do about her. I see her making the same mistakes I made, and I feel helpless to stop it.

Good mothers-in-law butt out is what Jane once told me, and I know that good mothers guide their children instead of lecturing them. For years I've butted out and shut up while Kate has barreled down the same path I took—being a woman who tends to everybody's needs except her own.

If it's not too late for me, then maybe it's not too late for Kate. Maybe the best thing I can do for her is set a shining example, be multifaceted instead of one-dimensional.

I take out my composition book and music transports me to creative vistas of the mind until my rumbling stomach reminds me that I didn't eat breakfast and all I brought to the beach is a pack of Nabs.

I'm peeling back the cellophane on my processed cheese and crackers when Ken and Irma show up with a picnic basket.

"When I saw you eating Nabs, I said, 'Ken, why don't we share our lunch with Beth?'"

"We hope you don't mind," Ken says. "Our children are scattered across five states and, except for our grandson, Adam, we don't get a chance to talk to many young people."

I almost burst into tears. Unexpected kindness always does that to me.

"That's very sweet. Are you sure I won't be intruding?"

"Of course not. I always cook enough for a logrolling." Irma passes the fried chicken. "We had six kids and I never got out of the habit."

Chicken is Howard's favorite food, and the first

time I ever attempted to fry it was on our first anniversary. Aunt Bonnie Kathleen taught me everything there was to know about books and art and music, but nothing at all about cooking. Her idea of a home-cooked meal was macaroni and cheese out of a box. Anyway, I used too much flour, too much heat and not enough oil. By the time Howard came home, the kitchen was filled with smoke, the charred remains of the chicken lay on a white platter and I was sobbing.

"There, there, now. It's not that bad." He'd kissed my tears, ate my chicken and told me it was delicious. Then he drew a bath, added bubbles and cleaned up the kitchen while I soaked away my misery. Afterward we made passionate love all over the house, including the kitchen table.

Suddenly the chicken clogs my throat, and when Ken pounds my back I burst into tears.

"Are you all right?" Irma asks, while I try to pull myself together, but the tides have pulled my emotions to the surface and my hurt tumbles out.

"I left my husband."

"Oh, well, now." Irma puts her arm around me while her husband looks at me with sympathetic dark eyes. "I left Ken once. When was it, darling?"

Amazement dries my tears.

"Nineteen forty-nine, sweetheart."

"I packed my bags and went down to the station and bought a ticket to Washington, D.C. By the time the train pulled in, Ken was sitting on the bench by me, his bags all packed. 'Going somewhere, toots?' he said, and we ended up going together."

"Had the time of our lives," Ken adds.

I picture me at that train station, wearing a fishtail suit and little red hat with a flirty veil, and Howard strolling casually by as if he's just come to pass the time of day. Suddenly, he's dipping me for a deep kiss, and we board the train and celebrate with sparkling champagne in the dining car.

"How did you manage to stay in love with each other all these years?"

"Passion," they answer together.

See, that's how a marriage ought to be.

"Respect and kindness, too," Irma adds. "We're always good to each other."

"And a whole lot of magic." Ken kisses Irma, and neither one of them is the least bit embarrassed that they have an audience.

It's not until we get to the peach pies that I learn she's a concert pianist and he's a magician. I tell them about my symphony, and by the time they get ready to leave we're exchanging addresses and phone numbers and promising to keep in touch.

I hope we will. Too often we lose the magic of these chance encounters by not following through. We immerse ourselves in the humdrum of daily living, thinking we'll call next week, and before you know it, it's Christmas and we've lost the address and can't even send a card.

Thinking of loss, I get so blue I'd be dragging my tail feathers if I had any. Why can't we hold on to the people who matter? It's these connections that weave the fabric of our lives.

"Listen," I tell them. "I'm going to be in Pensacola a while. I'd love to take both of you to dinner."

"Wouldn't that be lovely? Better yet, come to our house." Irma gives me directions to their beach house and we settle on tomorrow night at six; then I watch them walk toward home, arm in arm. Afterward, I work on my symphony until I am swallowed up by darkness.

Back at the Palm Breeze I put on my new nightshirt that reads Good Girls Have Haloes, Bad Girls Have Fun, and call Jane.

With Irma and Ken fresh on my mind I ask about my husband right off the bat.

"Have you seen Howard? Talked to him?"

"No."

"Has anybody else seen him?"

"Wait a minute, Beth. What's this about?"

I tell her what Grace said, and she says, "Grace York ought to be coated with peanut butter and hung out for the birds. Put your mind at rest. Howard's totally devoted to you."

"Hmm," I reply because if what Howard has been showing me is total devotion I'd hate to experience indifference.

"Have you seen Kate?" I ask.

"I was in the front yard cutting a bouquet of purple iris when she drove up early this evening. She was taking a chicken casserole to Howard."

"Did she seem depressed to you?"

"Oh, you know Kate. She's carrying on, as usual. She did tell me 'Somebody has to watch after poor Daddy.' But look on the bright side, Beth. Wouldn't you rather be doing something fantastic and brave than sitting home having your children call you *poor Mother?*"

"Right now I don't feel very fantastic and brave. I feel lonely. And scared."

"I'm coming down. I'll leave first thing in the morning."

"No. Wait. I really appreciate it, and I'd love to see you, but I need to do this by myself. If I'm the kind of woman who has to be propped up, then I might as well have stayed home."

"Way to go, girl. You've blazed the trail for all of us."

Jane has given me something good to hold on to, an image of myself as woman who's not afraid to go out on a limb to change things.

Tomorrow I'm going to continue with the small things I can easily change—eat healthy foods, finish my symphony, meditate. But I draw the line at exercise. God hasn't put diamonds on the floor yet, and the last time I looked I hadn't turned back into a twenty-year-old.

I climb into bed and automatically reach to the other side for Howard, but all I feel is an empty pillow. I'd better get used to that or else figure out a way to go home without continuing to be the only person in the house who knows where Howard's clean socks are.

CHAPTER 7

"Who made me Dr. Phil?"

—Kate

I was doing fine with the current situation until the casserole I'd meant to halve and take to Daddy bubbled up and ran all over the oven. Bonnie's the one who saw the smoke, and when she came running into the laundry room where I was sorting Rick's socks, yelling, "Mommy, Mommy, the house is on fire!" I nearly had a heart attack.

People my age do, you know. Especially women, because who else would take on the problems their mothers ran off and left behind? Nobody, that's who.

I jerked up my daughter and raced down the stairs, prepared to bolt out of the house and call 911 from the Crockett's next door, but all I saw was smoke coming out of the oven. No flames, thank goodness.

In as calm a voice as I could manage I assured my

daughter the house wasn't burning down, and then told her to run back upstairs and play. And now here I am up to my elbows in burnt burgundy beef.

If Mom were here I wouldn't have been putting double the ingredients in a casserole dish that turned out to be too small. Now, it's either hand-clean the mess so I can finish cooking it or turn on the auto-clean cycle and pick up dinner at Kentucky Fried Chicken.

I opt for hand-cleaning because Rick prefers home-cooked meals. Fitting on rubber gloves, I tackle the oven. But right in the middle of scrubbing I wonder how in the world I ended up with my head in the oven.

I was going to be a great designer. I was going to live in New York and make my mark on the fashion world with a line of clothes—most of them purple, my favorite color—that everybody would clamor for.

I wonder if Mom sacrificed her dreams to raise a family. Not that I'd trade Rick and Bonnie for a career; still…there are women who have it all. My college roommate, Kim, is a pediatrician as well as a wife and mother. And my friend Linda has her own beauty salon in Saltillo and a boyfriend named Stoker who wants to marry her and build her a house with a beauty shop attached.

Even my sister, Jenny, never backs down from a thing she wants.

By the time I emerge from the oven, I feel like a frazzled underachiever, which won't do at all. I don't believe in feeling sorry for myself. I chose this life and I'm happy with it. Most of the time.

By the time Bonnie and I get to Daddy's, he's already home. Daddy *never* leaves work early. Many a night I've seen Mom put his dinner in the warmer.

He looks terrible. His color's bad and he's hunched over like a very old man. I always considered Daddy ageless, in spite of his thinning hair and slight paunch. He has this kind of eternally youthful spring to his step and twinkle in his eye. Or used to.

I kiss his cheek while Bonnie climbs into his lap and wraps her arms around his neck.

"Daddy? Are you all right?"

"I am now." He smiles, but I can tell it's forced. "How are you, sweet pea?"

He tickles Bonnie under the chin and she giggles. If anybody passed by and looked in the window, they'd think this scene was perfectly normal. Well, I'm here to inform them it's not. There's not a single thing normal about this house now that it's empty of Mom.

"You two visit. I'm just going to put this casserole in the kitchen and your clean socks and underwear upstairs. Okay, Daddy?"

"I don't know what I'd do without you."

Poor Daddy. He says this every day when I come over. While I'm in the bedroom stowing his clean clothes, I turn back the bed the way Mom always did. Once when I asked her why she did it, she said, "It's a loving touch, one of the many small gestures that keep a marriage fresh."

I did the same thing for Rick until Mom left; I figured if she was wrong about the bed then maybe she was wrong about other things. I just can't figure out what.

When somebody has been your hero all your life, it's hard to turn around and think of them as fallible.

Before I go back downstairs I inspect everything to make sure the housekeeper is doing her job. Mom thinks Velma Lou is some kind of wizard. But once, after Velma Lou had supposedly cleaned, I found dust bunnies as big as baseballs under my bed, and she just laughed. Mom never was a stickler for order.

Things aren't perfect up here but they're passable so I head back downstairs.

"Daddy, do you need anything else before Bonnie and I go home?"

"Can you stay a minute, Kate? I need to talk to you. Privately."

"Sure. Bonnie, can you go to Papa's playroom and play with your toys?"

You never know how much a three-year-old will understand.

While she trots off with Rufus bounding along behind her—obviously glad to have somebody to play with—I glance at my watch. Rick will be home in thirty minutes, and I like to have time to touch up my makeup and greet him at the door with a kiss. Listen, I'm no dummy. His secretary, Cindi, was once Vardaman's Sweet Potato Queen, and I'm not fixing to suffer by comparison. Who knows? A well-groomed, pleased-to-see-you wife at the door could be the thing that keeps his mind off Cindi's sweet potatoes and other ample body parts and on his marriage.

I sink onto the sofa hoping this won't take more than ten minutes.

"When do you think your mother's coming home?"

"I don't know." Seeing the consternation on his face, I amend that. "Soon, probably."

"Do you think she wanted me to go charging after her, Kate?"

"I don't know. She hasn't told me much."

"I forgot her birthday last month. Do you think she's still mad? I made amends with a diamond brace-let. Shouldn't that have been enough?"

Good grief. Who does he think I am? Dr. Phil? Daddy's the one with Dr. in front of his name.

"She loved the bracelet, Daddy. I don't think that's what's bugging Mom."

He sits with his hands folded the way he used to when he was pondering something serious Jenny or I had done. I love this about my daddy—that he never flies off the handle. He simply mulls over a problem until he can come up with a solution.

Though, for the life of me, I can't see how he's going to figure out how to fix this mess our family is in. For goodness sake, what will we do if Mom's not back by the Fourth of July? We thrive on tradition, and we've always had a big family barbecue in the backyard—Daddy's baby back ribs and Mom's double-chocolate layer cake.

And I don't even want to think about Thanksgiv-ing and Christmas.

"Kate, what would make a woman stay away a week? The only thing I can figure out is another man."

"Oh, Dad..." I put my arm around his sagging shoulders. "I think Mom's searching for something she thinks she doesn't have, but it's certainly not another man. She's impulsive, but she would never do that."

Amazingly, Daddy smiles. Who can figure parents?

"She has pulled some stunts, hasn't she? Do you remember that time she came home from Wal-Mart with a pregnant teenager?"

"Do I ever."

I had to give up my room. For two weeks. Mom found this runaway pregnant girl crying in the toilet and said it would have been inhuman and cruel to leave her. When Daddy asked why she didn't call the authorities who know how to deal with that sort of thing, she'd said, "Why, Howard, you're the authority. Wouldn't it be kinder to counsel her and show her a little kindness for a while before turning her over to rank strangers?"

As if Mom, herself, were not a rank stranger. But then she's always had this winsome, openhearted way about her that attracts people. Jenny used to say Mom collected stray people like some folks collect lost cats and dogs.

Time is ticking away, and if I'm not out of here in the next five minutes I won't be home by the time Rick gets there.

"Is there anything else you want to talk about, Daddy?"

When he glances at the clock he gets this guilty look on his face, and I wish I hadn't said anything. Would it hurt Rick to come home to an empty house once in a blue moon?

"Hon, I'm sorry. You go on home. You're a good daughter…and a good wife and mother."

He kisses me on the cheek and then goes to fetch Bonnie. At the door I give him last-minute instructions on heating the beef burgundy, and then I try not to speed going home.

Of course, Rick's already there, pacing around the kitchen as if he's accidentally come to the wrong house and doesn't know what to do.

"There you are. I thought I was going to have to go out for dinner."

Suddenly, I'm irked. You'd think a man with as many degrees as he has would at least know how to take a casserole out of the warmer. Squashing down my anger, I kiss him on the mouth. The worst thing a woman can do is light into her husband about something insignificant the second he walks in the door.

"Dinner will be ready in just a minute. I was over at Daddy's."

"How is Howard?"

"Barely hanging on. I feel like calling Mother and making her tell me where she is, then bringing her home myself."

"If that's what you want to do, it's all right with me, of course, but I'm in the middle of the big hospital case, and it's nice to come home to a good, hot dinner."

For a minute I thought he was going to say it was nice to come home to me. I turn my back so he won't see my fallen expression.

First Daddy is upset, and now me. It's as if Mom's discontent is spilling over and catching up with everybody she left behind.

Rick comes up behind me and puts his hands on my shoulder.

"Is everything all right, hon?"

That's another thing. Why can't he call me *darling* or *baby* or *sweetheart* or any number of other endearments? *Hon* is what my parents call me.

Suddenly I want to cry on somebody's shoulder. But not my husband's. It's my mother's shoulder I long for.

"Everything's fine. Why don't you and Bonnie go hang out together while I get dinner on the table?"

When he goes off with our daughter—which is

exactly what I told him to do—I want to throw the casserole into the middle of my Mexican tile floor and smash it to smithereens.

If Mom doesn't come to home soon, somebody's going to have to cart me off in a straitjacket.

CHAPTER 8

"Romeo in a Hawaiian shirt."

—Beth

I feel like I'm fixing to give birth to Shamu, the whale, relieved that it's finally going to be over and terrified I won't be able to pull it off. I'm at the Price's beach cottage, dinner is over and they're expecting me to play my symphony.

Irma's baby grand is in the corner, and ordinarily, I'd be itching to get my hands on it, but not tonight when I have to debut my own music. Too, Irma once gave a concert in Carnegie Hall and the only concert I ever played was for a band parents' fund-raising benefit.

I stall for time.

"I'd love to hear you play, Irma."

"Go ahead, sweetheart," Ken says. "Play that song you were playing the night we met."

They met in Los Angeles, where Irma had been

called in as a last-minute substitute for the warm-up act before Ken's show at the Magic Castle. She launches into an elegant, wistful rendition of "Someone to Watch over Me," and he gazes at her with such raptness and love, I want to weep.

"I fell in love with her the first time I saw her," he says, almost whispering so he won't drown out the music. "She was the most spectacular woman I'd ever seen, dressed in black velvet, shoulders bare, skin like peaches and cream. She had on a rhinestone choker, and with the lights on it, her face and eyes looked like somebody had lit them from inside."

"You were mighty handsome yourself, darling," she replies, never missing a beat.

"When she saw me standing in the wings and smiled, I said to myself, I'm the luckiest man alive. I still believe that. After all these years."

Irma rises from the piano stool and touches my arm. "Your turn."

I place my hands on the keyboard and feel the goose bumps pop up on my arm. The opening movement is majestic and lives up to the title of the opus—*Soaring*. I wrote the notes many years ago when every day was filled with magic and I knew all the secret words.

The second movement loses steam while my hands falter and my spirits sink. Ken and Irma are still smiling, but I can tell they're only doing so out of politeness. If I were a stranger giving a tickets-only concert, they'd walk out of the room and demand a refund.

By the time I've finished I'm sweating profusely and greatly in need of a large alcoholic drink and a quiet place to cry. No razor blades allowed. No loaded guns and no ropes with a convenient rafter nearby.

Twenty years flushed down the toilet. This symphony should be named *Plodding*. That's exactly how this music feels. There's no excitement, no heart-touching poignancy, no rapture.

Shamu is in the room, stillborn, and I am bereft.

"It needs a little more work," I tell them.

"Just a little tinkering here and there." Irma is being generous. "But what an accomplishment. It takes more than talent to write a symphony. It takes dedication and discipline and passion."

She'd change her mind about discipline and dedication if she knew it took me twenty years to produce one lousy piece of music. And forget passion. *Soaring* is as flat as my breasts when I was thirteen and Twiggy, longing to be sixteen and Marilyn Monroe.

In fact it reflects my life in ways I'd never been

aware of—the tedious routine, the stuck-in-a-rut feeling I've had for the past few years. There's a symbiotic relationship between art and life, and if one lacks a grand sense of passion, so will the other.

Ken and Irma have kept passion alive, not only for life, but for each other. You can see it in the looks they exchange, the way they touch and kiss, the sweet, secret smiles they give each other. No doubt when I leave they will walk into their bedroom, close the door and dance in perfect step to the ancient music of love.

When I leave I'll be lucky to get home without driving my car into the nearest tree, which is my current state of mind.

After we say good-night and I get in the car, I tell myself to buck up. It's not the end of the world, but might as well be because the world has vanished behind a curtain of tears and my dreams have vanished in the space of one evening.

What will I do now?

Scuttle through the lobby without being noticed, for one thing. The second is take a Tylenol PM, climb into bed, pull the covers over my head and hope I fall asleep in the next three seconds. I don't want to talk to anybody, I don't want to see anybody and most of all I don't want to think.

But morning comes and I have to. I can't face the world, can't face Ken and Irma, and I no longer have an excuse to sit in a pink plastic chair on the patio and compose.

If I'm not a composer, what am I? Was my flight to Florida all for nothing?

I lie back down, shut my eyes and will myself to sleep again, but my body refuses to tolerate the selfish demands of my mind. I pop up, wound as tightly as a piano wire. No, not that. I don't deserve to use any words associated with music or musical instruments.

A clock. That's what I am, a clock about to explode from tightly wound parts.

The clock on the TV says 11:00 a.m. My stomach growls, but I'm not fixing to face people in a public place—perky waitresses and chatty busboys and nosy checkout girls. I don't want them to see a grown woman cry.

Searching the bedside table for breakfast/lunch I find a stale Twinkie and the letter I wrote to Howard. Munching and sniffing, I read it again. It's not bad. Maybe I ought to mail it. It might be the only accomplishment of my flight to independence and self-knowledge—finally speaking my mind, at least on paper.

Before I can change my mind, I dress and go to the post office incognito, big sunglasses hiding puffy eyes and my beach hat pulled low over my forehead. Afterward I drive, heading east on I-10 with nothing on my mind except escape.

Of course, there's no escape with a cell phone. Jenny and Kate call and ask me how I am. I tell them I'm fine without feeling the least bit guilty about lying. A parent doesn't have to explain everything to a child, especially if that parent hasn't figured out the answers yet.

At sunset I pull over at a little roadside seafood shack, order fried shrimp and think about loss, loss of dreams, loss of a marriage.

It's hard not to envy Ken and Irma. If I had that kind of joie de vivre there's no telling what wondrous music I could compose. Certainly I'd have a better marriage. If people that age—at least seventy—can keep love alive, why couldn't Howard and I?

Maybe they know some tricks I don't know, some secret little love rituals that add spark to their union. By the time I get back to the Palm Breeze, it's after eight, and I've decided to revive my sizzle by watching a pay-per-view adults-only movie.

Who knows? It might work. That late-night sex guru on *Ask Sue* recommends it. I heard her one night while Howard was out of town and I was flipping through TV channels.

Shoot, maybe I'll have a double scotch on the rocks and call with my own question. "Hello, it's me, Beth. I want to know how an out-of-shape, middle-aged woman who feels as sexy as a leftover squash casserole gets her husband to pay as much attention to her as he does the apple pie à la mode she served at dinner."

Bathed and decked out in my nightshirt that proclaims Good Girls Have Haloes, Bad Girls Have Fun, I stretch on top of the bedspread, armed with the remote control and a bottle of gardenia-scented lotion. Woman à la mode. Ready to be not only the dessert but the whole seven-course meal.

The screen is small, no more than seventeen inches, and I have to lean forward and squint to see, which spoils the mood I'd hoped to create. Then the movie starts and I instantly try to figure out the plot.

Major mistake. There is no plot. Just a couple of actors with collagen-enhanced bodies cavorting around in skimpy, provocative clothing.

If I dressed in an outfit like that Howard would tell me to go and put on some clothes.

Of course, this is not Howard we're talking about. This is a hunk with a Dasani bottle in his britches.

I stifle my giggles, tell myself to pay attention. This movie is not meant to be art, so I try to get into the mood by concentrating on the more prurient aspects. I admit to getting a bit hot when the Dasani bottle comes into view, but the minute they start making those fake sounds I crack up.

Nobody sounds like that. Or do they? Maybe this is the missing link between Howard and me. Maybe I ought to practice.

I try to imitate the actress and end up sounding like somebody choking on a chicken bone. By now I'm laughing so hard tears are obscuring my vision.

Which is not a bad thing. After I wipe them off and see what those two contortionist fools are doing, I completely lose it. I never knew sex could look so ridiculous when you're not the one doing it.

Why don't they put on their clothes? Why don't they have a conversation above third-grade level, then go into the bedroom and shut the door like civilized people?

This misguided, silly venture is too good not to share. I pick up the phone to call Jane.

"Beth? You sound funny. My goodness…are you *laughing?*"

I tell her about the movie, then say, "Listen," and hold the phone closer to the TV so she can hear.

"Good grrrief!"

Jane laughs in wonderful, full-blown abandon, and all of a sudden I'm homesick.

"I miss you," I say.

"Yeah, I miss you, too, Beth. So, when are you coming home?"

"I don't know. I left so fast, I didn't stop to figure out how I'd get back. You know…I didn't say to myself 'If Howard says this or I do that, I'll come home.' I'm in limbo down here."

"I'll come down and we'll drive back together, if that's what you want."

"That's sweet of you, but I don't think so. I really want my exodus to mean something more than losing weight and trying to find myself. I want this time apart to mean something important for Howard and me."

"You still love him, don't you?"

"Well…I suppose I do. See, that's what I'm talking about. I want to be able to say yes or no and really mean it. I want to have the same kind of grand passion Irma and Ken do."

After I tell her about the Prices, Jane says, "That's lovely, but rare. Most of us just settle for something in between."

"Why? That's what I want to know. Why can't we have it all?"

* * *

That night I dream that Howard has come down to whisk me home. In the throes of a youthful lust we fling our dream-enhanced bodies onto the bed and start making these *noises*. With the sounds of Edvard Grieg's Concerto in A Minor crashing around us, I unzip his pants and find the Eiffel Tower.

Good grief. Recalling the dream over a Sara Lee muffin eaten on the patio under my favorite palm, I nearly choke. I haven't found the Eiffel Tower down there since I went into the kitchen at midnight to get Kate a bottle, and Howard and I made love on top of the kitchen table.

Is that what my dream of going to Paris is all about? If so maybe I ought to just get Howard some Viagra and forget about jet lag.

Brushing the crumbs off my shorts, I go back inside and take stock. I'm out of snacks and running low on toothpaste. If I'm going to stay I'll need those things. Staying has the appeal of cogitation without interruption, but going home makes a certain kind of sense. Two of my biggest unresolved issues are in Tupelo—Kate and Howard.

I watch more than *Ask Sue* on TV. I've been known to quote Dr. Phil, and he'd be the first to point out that part of this process of becoming myself is going to be resolving all my issues.

I head to Wal-Mart and grab the necessities, then on impulse decide to ditch the Mamie Eisenhower look in swimwear and select a blue two-piece suit.

At the checkout counter I'm turned inside out by the wailing blues of B.B. King coming over the intercom. I've always had a visceral reaction to the blues, maybe because I grew up near the cradle and cut my teeth on the gut-punching melodies of Robert Johnson and T-Bone Walker. When I directed the junior high band, I gravitated toward the blues. Nothing filled me with more excitement than hearing a mournful trumpet bear down on the blue notes.

Could it be that all these years I've been laboring on the wrong song?

And what about Howard? Have I been putting my attention on the wrong man? Have we outgrown each other, drifted so far apart we can never find our way back?

I don't go to the part of the beach I usually frequent because I'm a coward. After my humiliation at the piano, I still can't face Ken and Irma. Instead I trudge to the Ice Cream Shack on the lee side of the dunes and order a single dip of praline pecan. Back outside in search of a table, I spot a vaguely familiar man in aviator sunglasses headed my way. With his tall build and thinning hair he could be my husband except for the clothes. Howard never wears Bermuda shorts, and his sunglasses are so out-of-date they look like something worn by Eddie Albert on *Green Acres*.

And Howard wouldn't be caught dead in a Hawaiian shirt. Most of them are loud, but this one is exceptionally garish—neon green, covered in huge parrots nesting in coconut trees.

I'm just about to take my first bite of ice cream when the man removes his sunglasses. *Good grief.* It *is* Howard. My first thought is, *What in the world has come over him?* and my second is, *I don't have a single place to run.*

Diving for the nearest table, I turn my back to Howard and start up a conversation with a startled mother and her two young daughters.

"My goodness, look how you've grown," I say to the cherubic blonde on my left. "You're just like my little boy, Ben, growing like a weed."

The little girl—about Bonnie's age, I'm guessing—stares at me openmouthed while ice cream drizzles down her chin.

"Here, let me help you with that." I start dabbing her chin.

Howard has moved down the beach now, which is a very good thing, because the young mother snatches the napkin.

"Who do you think you are? Get away from my children before I call security."

"I'm sorry. I didn't mean to upset you. There was somebody I didn't want to see coming this way. That's all."

She doesn't say a word, just starts gathering up her children and all their beach paraphernalia. Obviously this is one small family who won't become instant friends. And who can blame her? This is not the day and age where you can let complete strangers horn in on your ice-cream social.

Shame on me. I'm a grandmother. I should know better.

"Don't go," I tell her. "Please. I'm leaving."

I hurry away, chastising myself. I've ruined a perfectly nice outing for them instead of facing the music.

Anyhow, Howard might not have been looking for me. Why would he?

Maybe that wasn't even my husband. In this glare, I might have let my imagination run away with me.

But what if it was him and he really was looking for me?

I suppose a sensible woman would climb in her car and return to the motel to figure out exactly how she feels about this latest turn of events. A woman bent on mapping out a great future would sit down in a quiet place, make a list of her goals and the pros and cons of leaving versus staying, and then decide exactly what she wanted to do about a husband searching for his runaway wife.

But, of course, I'm not that kind of woman. If I were, I would never have run away in the first place. Like Howard said, I'd have settled this matter at home, with all parties involved.

Panting from exertion, my heart beating too fast, I head back to my beach towel and settle down with my latest book, *Chicken Soup for the Soul;* a belated attempt at self-improvement. Besides, I'm probably the only person on the planet who hasn't read it.

But the words "go in one ear and out the other," as my aunt Bonnie Kathleen used to say. I'm too excited to concentrate, too exhilarated, too pumped up on the idea that I'm a woman capable of turning her conservative, stodgy husband into Romeo in a Hawaiian shirt.

CHAPTER 9

"Is a bad toupee better than none?"
—Howard

I should have bought that toupee in Columbus. At least it would keep my bald spot from blistering.

The last time I was in Pensacola was when Elizabeth and I vacationed down here six years ago. I'd forgotten how hot it can be on the beach. But then, why would I remember? I stay cooped up in my office all day trying to earn a better-than-decent living.

Pausing under the nebulous shade of a scrubby beach pine, I wipe sweat off my face. It won't do to think about the negative aspects of a wife running away from a perfectly good husband who makes her a great living. If I'm going get into that mind-set, I might as well have stayed home.

Instead I concentrate on the task at hand: convincing Elizabeth to come home. I hope I'm not on a fool's

errand. It's not as if Elizabeth said anything in her letter to indicate she wants our marriage to work, but the
mere act of writing it shows that at least she's thinking
about me, about us.

Last night when Kate brought supper over, I
showed her the letter and asked her what she thought.
Now I wished I hadn't. She cried after she read it.

"Doesn't Mom know how wonderful we think she is?"

"I don't know," I told Kate, and at that moment I
felt like a complete failure. The best advice I give my
patients is to communicate. How could I have failed
to do it with the person who is most important to me?

"Maybe I just took her for granted," I said.

Suddenly I saw myself as a man who doesn't pay attention to the people who really matter, a rather self-
absorbed man who spends all his energies doing the
things he excels at—counseling patients and making
money—and very little at the things he doesn't do well.

"Dad, what are we going to do? What if Mom
doesn't come back?"

"We can't make her come home, but at least I'm
going to try."

Pride is the only thing that kept me from going after her in the first place. I wanted to blame somebody,
and so I blamed her. The truth about marriage is that

it can't be pinned down to right and wrong, your fault or mine. It's a chameleon, fierce and fragile, illusive, and yet if you treat it with just the right amount of respect, trust and awe, it will be the shining achievement of your life. Your heart. Your soul. Your life's blood.

That's what I've come to Florida to tell Elizabeth.

That's also why I stopped in Columbus and bought these absurd clothes and these silly sunglasses. I want her to know that I'm willing to make changes.

Of course, the other reason is that I'm afraid she's run off with a yuppie beach-boy type, and if I have any hope of winning her back, I've got to compete. Show I can be hip, too. Show I've still got a little fire in the belly.

The young salesgirl in the mall (Glo, her name tag read) reminded me of Kate at that age. About nineteen, I'd say. Probably a student at the "W." She was so sweet and friendly I told her about my wife leaving me and the purpose of my trip, and that's when Glo suggested the toupee.

"They have really nice ones at Wigs and Things on the south side of the mall. A toupee would take ten years off your age."

It was the toupee business that brought me to my

senses. I've never confided in strangers; that's something Elizabeth does. I guess the thought of finding my wife with another man robbed me of common sense as well my sense of style. Anyhow, after I embarrassed myself by discussing toupees with a rank stranger, I shut up about my personal life.

Now that I'm here on the beach, I'm having second thoughts about the Hawaiian shirt. I don't see another one like it. Maybe I should have stuck with the one that had palm trees.

And why didn't I remember sunscreen? My legs and the top of my head are burning to a crisp. I've only been here forty minutes, and already my legs look like lobsters. Why didn't I wait at the Palm Breeze? That would have been the sensible thing to do. But, of course, Elizabeth's rash flight knocked everything in my life askew, including my judgment.

Lucky for me, instead of calling all over town, I still had enough sense to figure out that Elizabeth would stay at the Palm Breeze. She loved it when we were down here before.

I like to think that in thirty years together I've learned to predict my wife's erratic ways. And I could until she ran off without so much as a "fare you well."

That was a nice young man at the check-in, but I

don't think he'd have told me a thing if I hadn't said I had come down as a surprise for my wife. Thankfully, I'm a good judge of people. He's a romantic. I could tell by the romantic ballad he was listening to.

I'm heading back to the Palm Breeze if I don't find Elizabeth in the next ten minutes. It's so miserably humid sweat's running out of my eyebrows and streaking my sunglasses.

I wipe them off and then stroll back toward the parking lot, scanning the beach. If Elizabeth had brought her old blue bathing suit, I'd have spotted her in a minute. But *no*, she had to fly off and leave everything behind.

She's impulsive by nature, the exact opposite of me, but I guess that's one of the things that attracted me in the first place. The day I met her I'd driven from Oxford with my college buddies Curt Haines and Russell Weaver for a weekend on the Gulf Coast, and Elizabeth Holt was the first person I saw.

Or so it seems all these years later. In retrospect, I must have seen dozens of people before I stopped at Gus Stevens's restaurant for his famous fried oysters. And there she was, sitting at a table with a bunch of rowdy, beach-boy types, scarfing down oysters on the half-shell while they counted.

"Damn," Curt said. "That girl's going to make her-self sick."

"She'll stop before that," I said, not knowing Eliz-abeth.

We ordered beers and fried shrimp and oysters, and I made sure I took a seat across from her so I could watch. Lord, that woman fascinated me, even then.

Of course, she didn't stop eating until she'd won whatever bet they'd placed. When she waved good-bye and bounced outside, I could see she was going to be sick, so I excused myself and went after her.

She was standing under a live oak tree, losing the contents of her stomach. I pulled a clean white hand-kerchief out of my pocket. "Here. Looks like you could use this."

And that's how it started with Elizabeth and me—her leaping before she looked, and me always there to pick up the pieces.

Now she's nowhere in sight. Discouraged, I'm about to head back to my car when suddenly I spot this woman holding a book, head tilted exactly the way Eliz-abeth always does when she's concentrating. I skirt around the towel, out of her view, I hope, trying to be discreet.

This woman is slimmer than Elizabeth, and

tanned. Also, the swimsuit is two-piece, not at all the type she wears. And yet, when she starts nibbling on her right index finger—a years-long habit she has when her emotions are deeply involved—I know without a doubt that I've found my wife.

Relief washes over me. She's alone. There is no buff beach boy, no tanned jock in one of those ridiculous bathing suits that shows what a stud he is.

Of course, that doesn't mean she won't have one stashed back at the motel. I should have asked the guy at the check-in counter.

Suddenly I'm overcome with uncertainty. What will I say to her? How will she react?

It doesn't take long to find out. She looks up and spots me.

"Howard."

That's all she says, just *Howard*, and then she stares at me as if she's trying to recall exactly who I am. She makes me feel like a squirming schoolboy. I guess it's those blue eyes of her, so clear they reflect the sky and the water and seem to be looking straight inside me.

"Hello, Elizabeth."

"Is that all you can say?"

I guess it is or I would have thought of something that wouldn't get her hackles up right off the bat.

Clearly, I should have taken another day or two to map out a plan before I hauled myself down here.

"What do you want me to say?" Two bright red battle flags dot her cheeks, and if I don't turn this conversation around soon, she's going to storm off—and not to our bedroom where I could make the peace. "You look nice, Elizabeth."

She gives me the once-over, and all of a sudden she starts laughing. Who can figure women?

Although I don't see a thing funny about this situation, I smile to show I'm a good sport and that I get it...whatever *it* is.

"Here I am parading around half-naked, and there you are in that god-awful Hawaiian shirt. Aren't we a pair?"

"I guess we are," I say, hoping she means that in a good way.

She swings her newly tanned legs, and I can't help but notice how nice they look, how nice she looks—younger, livelier, almost like the girl I fell in love with more than thirty years ago. For the first time in weeks, maybe even months, I feel the stirrings of an arousal. The intensity of it takes me by surprise.

I don't know whether my renewed sexual interest is due to our long absence or being in a new place or my wife's new youthful glow, but I'm not going to look this particular gift horse in the mouth. I start looking for a place to make out.

"Let's go somewhere where we can be alone."

When I take her hand to pull her up, she bumps against me and actually blushes.

"Why, Howard…"

"Yeah…well, babe, it's been a long time. And if I don't get moving I soon won't be able to."

"Let's take my car," she says. "We can come back for yours later."

Both of us are jogging toward the parking lot like horny teenagers in the first rush of lust. I feel rejuvenated, as well as vindicated and relieved. Obviously if she has another man he can't measure up. Equally obvious, I don't have to even ask, which is a relief.

Sometimes I don't know what to say to Elizabeth. Maybe seeing patients all day depletes my well of wisdom, and by the time I get home I don't have anything left to say. Besides, shouldn't she know me by now? Shouldn't she know that my intentions toward her are always good?

"Shoot," she says.

Elizabeth's so flustered she drops her keys, and they bounce under the car. Getting on all fours with an erection the size of a flag pole is no easy feat. Fortunately I don't have to crawl under the car: my arms are long enough and I snag the keys on the first attempt.

"Hurry, Howard."

Sweating profusely, I heave myself upright, but not before I notice how trim and perky her feet and ankles look. When we get back to the motel, maybe I'll start there. I've read that some women like that. If kissing Elizabeth's feet is what it takes to get her back, I'm willing to give it a try.

CHAPTER 10

"Can love survive being stuck in a zipper?"
—Beth

Here I am in the Palm Breeze, tangled up in the pink chenille bedspread and Howard's pants. My swimsuit bottoms and our shoes landed somewhere near the door, but he came out of the gate too soon and now his zipper's stuck.

"Shift a little to the left, Howard."

I give a yank at his pants and he howls as if I've castrated him.

"What's wrong? I say.

"The belt buckle! Watch the belt buckle."

"Hold on. Let me just…"

I fumble between us, but the more I try to fix the zipper the more hopelessly we become entangled. Now his belt buckle is sawing against the inside of my leg.

"Is it working?" he pants. "Can you push them down?"

"I think so. Lift your left leg...now your right..."

"I can't. I'll be levitating."

Somewhere between his yowl of pain and my struggle with the stubborn Bermudas, we've lost our fire. What started out as a passionate assignation in the afternoon worthy of an X-rated movie has turned into a Groucho Marx movie.

"Elizabeth?" Howard lifts on his elbows and looks down at me. "I don't see what's so funny."

"Think about it."

He starts grinning, and all of a sudden we're sitting on the side of the bed, laughing so hard we're both crying.

"Why don't I get out of these pants and we'll start over?"

Recapturing the mood proves to be more than we can handle. He can't get it up and I can't get it on.

"I'm sorry, Elizabeth. I just don't know..."

"We've both had too much sun. Why don't we get something cool from the drink machine and sit on the patio?"

In side-by-side plastic chairs, we keep giving each other self-conscious looks. I can tell he's embarrassed that he couldn't perform, and truth be known, I'm a bit chagrined because I couldn't turn him on again.

In addition, I don't know what to say to him. Clearly we need to discuss marital issues, but shouldn't we have done that before our pell-mell rush to the bed? Of course, sex is a lovely Band-Aid to plaster over problems, but once you get in that cozy, just-you-and-me-babe mood, it's hard to regain the cool perspective you need to work through the issues.

Finally Howard says, "We can leave tonight."

I guess the surprise shows on my face because he clears his throat and then looks at me with those big brown puppy-dog eyes that I used to find irresistible. It's moments like this that make me wish I had a crystal ball. If I knew what the future held for us, I could move boldly in one direction or the other, but life's a guessing game. You just keep putting one foot in front of the other and hoping you don't stumble into too many sinkholes and bear traps.

"Or...if you want to, we'll wait till morning."

"Let me think a minute, Howard."

Now what? After dragging him to my bed like some horny teenager, how can I say I'm not sure I want to go?

Howard's never done anything as impulsive as dash off to Pensacola to retrieve a wayward wife. And the

Hawaiian shirt…goodness gracious. I feel wonderful and a bit powerful that I'm still capable of provoking my usually stodgy husband to these radical (for Howard) actions.

Besides, hadn't I already halfway decided to go home anyway to work out my issues?

Still, I have to know that I'm not stepping backward, just going back to the same old life.

"Howard, why did you come here?"

My question takes him aback. He hates introspection more than any man I've ever known. I don't know how he ended up in psychiatry.

"It was your letter. I didn't know how you felt until I read it, and I'm going to try to pay more attention."

His answer isn't the grand passion of Ken and Irma, but at least it's a start.

I gaze across the palms trying to visualize my future, but all I can see is a wasteland of cars baking in the heat on an acre of concrete in front of that icon of commercialism. All of a sudden I don't want to spend another day waking up to a view of Wal-Mart.

Howard takes my silence for hesitation.

"Elizabeth, why don't we go to a nice restaurant tonight and just relax? Maybe that Japanese restaurant you liked so much the last time we were here.

Or we'll get seafood, if that's what you prefer. Just tell me what you want."

How can I tell Howard what I want when I don't even know myself? Choosing a restaurant is not a problem, but choosing a life is daunting.

"Japanese is fine."

"Great! Then, after a good night's rest, we can leave for home."

"Okay," I say.

Sometimes you get swept along by events, and the best you can do is just breathe and try to float.

PART TWO

CHAPTER 11

"What lunatic said just kiss and make up?"
—Beth

If you could elaborate on the problem, Elizabeth, I'll try to fix it."

"Why don't we just relax a bit and build on what we started in Pensacola?"

Howard's face flushes, and I know what he's thinking. He couldn't start anything, and I didn't prove to be the great seductress who could make it happen.

Surrounded by our vast collection of books, the last rays of sunset slanting through French doors, glasses of Chardonnay in our hands, we look like a couple settling in for a quiet evening of holding hands and cozy conversation instead of two people facing each other across a marital battlefield. Howard calls it a summit conference and I call it torture. Instead of constantly analyzing, why can't we just *be*?

I take a fortifying sip of wine. We just got home an hour ago and now I know how the prodigal son must have felt when he returned home. Grateful and guilty at the same time.

"There's no time like the present," Howard said.

"I hate it when you do that."

"Do what?"

"Speak in platitudes."

"Is that one of the reasons you ran away? Because you don't like the way I talk?"

"Please, Howard. Give me more credit than that. And I didn't *run away*. I just left, that's all."

"That's all? Leaving me stranded without a clue is no small thing, Elizabeth."

We've only been in the library (as Howard calls it) less than five minutes, and already I'm on the defensive.

"I hate it that you call this the library," I tell him. "Why can't you just call it the den, like ordinary people?"

"That's the second time you've used the word *hate*. And both in reference to the way I speak."

When he goes the desk, gets a pad and pencil, and starts jotting notes, I want to scream. He's always done this—made lists and notes and itineraries. Why did I ever think his meticulous ways were endearing?

"This is not simply about you, Howard. It's about us. And stop analyzing everything I say. I feel like one of your patients."

Wine sloshes over the rim of my glass as I huff toward the French doors. I try to find hope in the view, but all I can feel at the moment is frustration. Even Aunt Bonnie Kathleen's favorite platitude—Rome wasn't built in a day—doesn't help.

"Elizabeth?" Howard puts a hand on my shoulder, then pulls it back. "I'm sorry."

Why didn't he leave it there? Why does he back off from touching me?

"Me, too," I say, turning around to face him.

"I just want us to go back to what we had, Elizabeth."

"I don't want to go backward, Howard. I want to go forward to something more exciting and more wonderful. I want us to be like Ken and Irma."

When I tell him about the Prices, he gets very quiet. Over the years Howard has developed this inscrutable face. I never can figure out what he's thinking.

Finally he says, "I thought that's what we had, Elizabeth."

Lord, haul me off to the loony bin now. If he thinks

this parched desert of a marriage is wonderful, then I don't see how we're ever going to find any middle ground. What else can I say to make him see?

When my old, faithful Lab Rufus wanders in and rubs against my legs to be patted, I get on my knees and greet him as if he's a St. Bernard who has rescued me from a frozen mountain. Here's something I can do that doesn't involve a major, heart-wrenching decision.

"It's too beautiful to stay inside," I say. "Let's take Rufus for a walk."

"Why didn't you tell me you'd rather be in the garden?"

"I just did."

"If you'd said something earlier, maybe we could have avoided all this drama."

This is the point where one of us always stomps off to pout, and the other waits a suitable cooling off period (generally an hour or two) before coming forth with a conciliatory gesture (usually a hug, sometimes a peck on the cheek). If we're going to fall back into that pattern, I might as well have stayed in Florida.

"Listen, Howard. I don't want to argue with you, and I don't want to sit around performing a postmortem on our marriage."

"Is that what you think this is? A postmortem?"

"That's what it feels like."

Stricken and genuinely puzzled, he rakes his hands through his thinning hair, and then picks up his notes and walks toward the door like a very old man. I want to pat him on the head and say, *There, there.*

"Howard. Wait."

"If you have something to say, I'm listening."

I start to yell, *Why didn't you just say I'm listening?* but then realize that if he'd been the one to leave me I'd want answers, too.

Suddenly chilled by this too-cool house, this too-cool marriage, I wrap my arms around myself.

"I can't identify exactly what's wrong with us," I add. "All I know is that I don't feel connected to you anymore. It's as if we came to a crossroads and you went right while I went left."

"That doesn't give me much to go on."

I feel as if I'm banging my head against a wall. Howard wants to solve us the way he would a cross-word puzzle. How can you fix a marriage with logic?

Of course, I'm the one who wants change. Am I expecting too much or is he expecting too little?

"Were you happy the way things were between us, Howard?"

"I never noticed anything wrong." He paces to the

bookshelves and back. "I don't get it, Elizabeth. How do you expect me to fix something if I don't know what's wrong?"

"Don't you see, Howard? It's not up to you to fix it. It's up to both of us to try to find a way back to each other."

"I don't know where to start. At least give me some idea of what you want, Elizabeth."

"I want to walk in the sunset. Holding hands. We don't do that anymore. Just touch each other."

"Is that all?"

I have a hard time controlling a sigh. If I could type up a list of grievances, Howard would address them all within the next two days, then check them off, item by item.

"Why don't we start there and try to build on it, Howard?"

It's cool in the garden, and the air holds a hint of rain. I've always loved this time of year before the heat and humidity suck the life out of every living thing. This is the season of bloom and newness, lush green growth and promise.

While Rufus bounds joyfully along sniffing out fun, we walk side by side, hands linked, hips touching and I remember Ken and Irma, the beauty of their union, the passion always simmering just beneath the surface. I'm not sure Howard and I ever had what they do, and I certainly don't know if we can find it. But this much I do know: I'm willing to try.

The New Dawn roses are spectacular, hanging in full pink bunches over the wrought-iron arbor in our backyard. I lean over to inhale the fragrance, then pluck one and tuck it behind my ear.

Seized by an impulsive madness I arch my arms over my head, twirl around and shout, "Olé!"

Howard's tight, almost-embarrassed smile stops me in my tracks.

"What?" I ask. "What is it?"

"About last night, Elizabeth…"

"Let's not talk it to death, Howard. Let's just enjoy the roses." Some things are best left unsaid until the trauma of the event wears off.

We continue our stroll of the garden, but we're no longer holding hands. So much for our great start. Of course, things might have been different between us if last night at the Palm Breeze had turned out differently.

After our failed attempt at madcap romance in the heat of afternoon, we had a pleasant enough meal at Iamato's restaurant, not discussing anything more significant than the dance class Kate found for Bonnie.

When we got back to the Palm Breeze, Howard and I watched the ten o'clock news then attempted to recapture an amorous mood, but nothing happened down south. For either of us.

"Maybe if we put on some romantic music…" I said.

I found a station on the radio that played classic romantic ballads, and then crawled back under the covers while Peggy Lee crooned "That Old Black Magic." After fifteen minutes we were both covered in sweat, but not the magic kind—the nervous kind. Nothing kills passion more than trying too hard.

Not wanting to hurt his feelings, I faked a yawn and said, "Well, good night, Howard."

"Wait, Elizabeth…" He fumbled around between us some more. "Let me just…"

I felt like a cantaloupe in the produce section of the supermarket. You know those women who come along and thump every one of the melons trying to find the ripest? Well, let me tell you, there wasn't an inch of my body that Howard didn't *thump*.

Mercifully, he gave up after another ten minutes of embarrassment. Now, I'm not one of those shallow women who judge a husband based merely on sex, but I do happen to believe it's the glue that holds everything else in the marriage together. When you've got that just-loved feeling, it's easy to overlook small irritations and take major problems in stride. But everything around you can get tinged gray and ugly if you're constantly frustrated and deprived.

The last rays are fading from the garden, and by the time we finish our stroll I'm already dreading tonight. Not a good sign. Egos are fragile things. I don't know if Howard's can survive another debacle…or mine either, for that matter.

Every woman wants to think of herself as the kind of femme fatale who can drive a man to his knees with desire. Shoot, I'd settle for being a moderately appealing woman who rouses a man to action even if the equipment is half-cocked.

Inside, Howard heads for his favorite chair and flicks on the six o'clock news while I hover in the doorway.

Belatedly he turns off the television and says, "We can eat out if you'd like."

"No, that's okay. I'll cook."

It's a small way of showing my commitment to making our marriage work. Besides, I enjoy the kitchen, love the scent of spices and the look and feel of shiny copper pots. Jane's the same way. I subscribe to *Gourmet*, she subscribes to *Southern Living*, and we meet over morning coffee to exchange recipes. Old-fashioned, I know. Still, there's an art to cooking if you do it right.

The downsides of cooking are the constancy and the expectations of those waiting to be fed.

I flip through my back issues of *Gourmet* looking for Howard's favorites, chicken cordon bleu and pear pie. I'll do both if I have the right cheeses. Who knows what my refrigerator holds after my extended absence?

More than cheese, I can guarantee you that. The shelves are groaning with leftovers, every casserole in Kate's culinary repertoire artfully displayed in the rainbow-colored plastic storage containers she got at a wedding shower. There's enough food in here to feed a small third-world country for three days.

Kate made certain her father didn't miss me at all.

Knee-jerk anger propels me to the phone, but by the time I've dialed her prefix, my anger has fizzled. If I'd had a father under similar circumstances, wouldn't I have done the same thing? And besides, at least I know that Howard didn't drive all the way to the coast because he missed my cooking.

I put the receiver back in its cradle and the chicken in the oven. By the time I'm wrist deep in pastry, the phone rings. I give it three rings to see if Howard is going to answer, and when he doesn't, I pick up and say hello.

Dead silence. "Hello," I say again.

"I was expecting Daddy."

"He's watching TV. How are you, Kate?"

Standing in a kitchen cozy with colored light from a Tiffany shade and heat from the oven, I feel the chill of not knowing how to bridge the gap between us.

"Are you home to stay, Mom?"

"I wish I could give you a definitive answer, but I honestly don't know. It depends."

"If it depends on Daddy, he wants you to stay."

"Oh, Katie…I've missed you, and I want to stay, really I do. But it's not that simple."

"Mom…please…I don't want to talk about this anymore. Can you put Daddy on?"

Feeling as if I'm suddenly an outsider in my own family, I deliver the message to Howard.

"Telephone."

"Who is it?"

"Kate."

When he picks up the phone I'm tempted to eavesdrop, but pride won't let me. All I hear as I walk back toward the kitchen is my husband explaining to my daughter that "the trip went as well as could be expected for a spur-of-the-moment decision."

As if I'm an afterthought. As if he has to consult Kate on whether I'm worth the drive to Pensacola. As if she's the one who has the say in our marriage.

I slam my fists into the dough as if it's my worst enemy. Not until I shove the pear pie into the oven do I realize I'm crying. Silently.

Well, I have news for my daughter. I have no intention of letting her or anybody else make the decisions around this household. The last time I looked I was still Howard's wife, and by George, that's the way it's going to stay until one of us decides to change it.

Furthermore, it's nobody's business but ours what goes on between us. Marriage is private. Even from children.

Finally, I sag onto the kitchen stool, felled by the realization that I've come home to an unholy mess. And not just with my older daughter, either. Not a thing has changed between Howard and me. He's watching TV and I'm making dinner, and neither of us has a clue what the other really wants or needs. After all these years!

I fish around in my purse for my cell phone.

"Jane, I'm home."

"I saw your car come in. I would have come right over, but I figured you and Howard had things to discuss."

"Can I come over in the morning and talk?"

"I'll have a coffee cake hot."

Women would kill for a best friend like Jane. Feeling better already, I set the dining room table with my best china and silver, then light candles and select Mozart and Beethoven and Debussy, music guaranteed to soothe jangled nerves.

If Howard's as uptight as I am, this evening does not look promising.

CHAPTER 12

"How can you be a hero if your white stallion
is a jackass?"

—Howard

Elizabeth's cooking two of my favorite dishes, chicken and pear pie. I guess I ought to take that as an indication that things are going to be all right between us, but after last night, I'm having doubts about everything. Including my own masculinity.

What's wrong with me? I went all the way to Florida to get Elizabeth—who's looking better than I've seen her in years, by the way—and still I couldn't perform. On top of that, my stomach's growling from hunger and the delicious aromas coming from the kitchen are making my mouth water; and I'm sitting here like a rabbit in a hole, scared to get out of this chair and face my own wife.

It must be the approach of bedtime that has me paralyzed. Fear. That's what I'd tell my patients, but darn it all, I never thought I'd have to question my own motives.

"Howard. Dinner's ready."

I jerk like a guilty schoolboy. Elizabeth's standing in the doorway, and now there's nothing I can do except follow her to the dinner table and try to make conversation without tripping over my own tongue. I don't know what to say to her anymore. When did that happen? After she left or before?

She's set the table with our good china and even lit candles. If she's trying to create a romantic mood, she's failed. What she's created is panic. Expectations I can't seem to fulfill. Performance pressure.

It's not her fault, though. Maybe none of this is. Maybe I need to make an appointment with my colleague Jack Warner and have my own head examined. Obviously I'm doing something wrong or a generous-hearted, undemanding person like Elizabeth would never have left.

"This looks delicious," I tell her.

"Thank you."

We fall into an uneasy silence like two people who've been set up on a blind date and can't decide whether it's a big joke or whether it will turn out to be the best thing that ever happened to them.

"Howard…" she begins, and I nearly drop my fork.
"Yes?"

"I was just thinking."

I wait, hoping for a revelation, but she starts arranging her food in separate little piles in her plate, making sure the beans don't touch the corn. She's always done that, refused to mix her food. I used to think it was cute. Now I want to jerk the fork out of her hand and tell her just to eat her food like a grown-up.

After I get myself under control, I say, "What were you thinking, Elizabeth?"

"About redecorating the house."

Is that all? I don't know whether to be relieved or mad. Surely she didn't leave me because she was tired of the way the house looks.

"Well, sure, honey. Whatever you want."

This pisses her off, and she puts down her fork real slow. Now what?

"What do you want, Howard?"

"What do you mean, what do I want?"

"Do you like the house the way it is, or would you be upset if we changed the colors?"

To be quite frank with you, I never even notice. If you asked me the color of my own bedroom, I'd be hard-pressed to say. I don't really care, for that matter, but I can see this is not the response Elizabeth's looking for. I wrack my brain trying to think of something noninflammatory to say, but I'm as lost as if she'd asked me to design a rocket ship. What do I know about decorating?

"What color did you have in mind, hon?"

"Purple."

Great-granny in a nightshirt! A purple room. Guaranteed to produce nightmares and maybe even insanity.

"Why not something more soothing? Say blue. Or beige."

Uh-oh. She pushes her plate back and gets out of her chair with the painstaking slowness of an ancient arthritic.

"For your information, Howard, the house is already blue and beige."

She marches stiff-backed to the kitchen, and I don't know whether to shit or go blind, as the old saying goes. Well, she asked and I told her. She can't have it both ways. She either wants the truth, or she doesn't.

Should I follow her into the kitchen and try to smooth things over, or sit here and finish my pear pie? To tell the truth, I'd as soon tangle with a crosscut saw as corner her in the kitchen, so I finish my pie.

I sit there a while waiting for her to come back, but obviously she's abandoned me to the wretched contemplation of living an unobservant life. If Elizabeth had as many patients' problems to observe and rectify as I do, she'd come home and sink in her chair just grateful for the cushion. She wouldn't care if the walls were blue or purple or turd brindle.

What I feel like doing is standing up and shouting, "Just paint the whole damn house purple and be done with it," but that would be the end of marriage as I know it.

And, hell, what do I know? Nothing, it looks like.

Except that this whole unfortunate interlude is driving me to think in curse words. I'm not the kind of man who uses foul language. In my opinion only the uneducated or the lazy do that. There are too many wonderfully descriptive words to resort to gutter language.

The clock that belonged to my great-grandfather Martin chimes eight times in the hallway. Two and a half more hours until P.T.—Performance Time.

If I didn't have to go in the kitchen where Elizabeth is, I'd pour myself another cup of coffee and sit here trying to figure the best course of action. Why can't she be like other women and plead a headache? At least, every now and then?

In our thirty years together she's never refused sex. Not even that time she had flu and could hardly hold her head off the pillow. Why she turned me on is a mystery, and why I even approached her under the circumstances is an even greater one. But she didn't refuse me, and it was some of the sweetest sex we've ever had. Tender. Beautiful.

Maybe I'll tell her I've got work to do. That might fly. After all, I took two days off traipsing down to Florida to get her.

"Howard?"

She's in the doorway looking normal. I can always tell whether she's in control by her facial expression and her body language. One of her truly endearing qualities is that Elizabeth lacks subterfuge.

Of course, she fooled me completely with this running away business, but I'm hoping that was an oversight on my part. Something I'd have seen in her face if I hadn't been so busy trying to keep Glenda Mac-Intyre from committing suicide and Rachel Freeman from starving herself to death.

"I'm sorry I flew off the handle," she says.

"That's okay."

"It was trivial. I guess I'm just trying too hard for an instant fix."

She runs her fingers through her hair. I've always loved it when she does that. She has this thick, glossy hair that feels like the pelt of a very healthy animal. I guess there are more romantic ways to describe it, but that's the best I can come up with. When it comes right down to it, I guess I'm not a very romantic guy.

She's still standing in the doorway, and I get up and put my arm around her shoulder. She leans into me a bit, and we just stand there, holding on.

I'm not fooled, though. Fixing what's wrong with our marriage is not going to be this easy.

"Howard?"

"Hmm?"

"After I finish the dishes let's just sit on the sofa together and hold hands. Do you mind?"

Hold hands? We haven't done that since we were dating. I'm not sure I even remember how.

"No, I don't mind."

When she glances up I see a flash of disappointment, and I figure I've just put my foot in my mouth again. Why do women make such a big deal out of stuff like holding hands?

"That would be great, Elizabeth."

"Good."

She heads back to the kitchen and belatedly I follow.

"Need any help in here?"

"No, I'm fine."

"Okay, then. See you in a bit."

I wander toward my favorite chair, and then jump up, guilty. Should I be sitting on the sofa waiting for her or should I get up and join her when she comes in? How ridiculous to be stymied by ordinary things. Things I used to take for granted. I feel like somebody from Mars who has just stumbled to Earth and doesn't know the least thing about human behavior.

Furthermore, my heart feels funny. If I have a heart attack in the middle of all this, maybe Elizabeth will get her mind off purple walls and holding hands and onto things that really matter, like being able to sit down in your favorite chair after a good meal and fall asleep, or for that matter, enjoying the meal without worrying about whether you can get it up in the bedroom afterward.

"Howard? Is anything wrong?"

Lord, there she stands staring at me as if I've lost the last hair on my head. I reach up just to make sure. My bald spot feels two inches bigger than it did yesterday, but all this stress is enough to make you lose your hair.

"No, nothing," I say. "Why?"

"Well, you're just standing there in the middle of the floor looking funny. I thought maybe you were sick."

Come to think of it, there's an idea. If you're sick, how can you be expected to go charging around like some pheromone-fueled hero when you know full well your white stallion has turned to a jackass?

And so I tell her, "Just a touch of indigestion, that's all."

First swearing and then lying. What next? I never knew there were so many levels a desperate man could sink to.

"I'll get you some Tums."

My relief when she leaves the room is short-lived because I know she's coming back. With antacid tablets that taste like chalk. It's my own darned fault that I'll have to suck it up and eat them anyway. That's what I get for lying.

I hear the sound of a cabinet door slamming and then staccato tapping on the hardwood floor. She always walks like that when she's in a hurry or irritated. I'm hoping for the former.

Before she gets back I sink onto the sofa and put my feet on the coffee table, trying to act as if I'm relaxed and settling in for an ordinary evening.

She hands me the tablets and I start chewing.

"I hope it wasn't the chicken," she says.

"Of course not. I've had a lot on my mind. That's all."

There's a shawl draped across the back of the sofa for no good reason that I can think of, and she fiddles with the fringe.

"I guess I'm the cause," she says.

"Well, some, but work's been a bear."

"Oh."

I don't talk about my patients and she never pries, but when you're casting around to think of something to say to your practically estranged wife and the subject of work is off limits and sex is a land mine waiting to blow your prized body parts off, it's hard to come up with a viable alternative.

Finally she says, "Do you want to watch TV?"

I leap up and turn it on before she can change her mind. There's some insipid comedy with a laugh track playing, and I try to act as if I'm enjoying the show, but out of the corner of my eye I can see her stiff-necked posture.

What am I doing wrong now? All of a sudden I remember that she wanted to hold hands. I reach out and take hers, but it lies in mine like a dead fish, so I guess she's changed her mind. Clearly, if I want this marriage to succeed I'm going to have to take up mind reading.

I sit through the comedy and some inane detective show hanging on to my wife's hand with all the passion of somebody hooked up to life support. Shouldn't there be more to this? Shouldn't I be feeling the fires that lead to foreplay or at the very least a little tingle that might lead to some nice hugging and kissing?

What I feel is defeated. And I guess she does, too, because when she says, "I'll make us some coffee," I don't tell her to stay.

Everything starts settling back to normal when she leaves. Feeling like a car running on overdrive too long, I sag against the cushions and close my eyes.

The next thing I know, I'm waking up with cotton in my mouth, a dull throbbing behind my eyes and the guilty realization that I fell asleep on the sofa and left my wife to climb the stairs to our bedroom with nobody except the dog. I guess that's one way to get out of having to face the possibility of sexual humiliation, but it's also a surefire way to send the wrong message to a wife who has already run away once.

What if she does it again? I snap on the lamp and glance at my watch. Six o'clock. Too late to climb into bed with her and try to make up for not sleeping there last night. Besides, I can't afford to miss my eight o'clock appointment. My patients depend on me, and at least in that arena, I can shine.

Of course, if I were one of my patients I'd take my own advice and hustle up the stairs and talk to my wife. I'm halfway up the stairs when I realize that I don't have enough time for any meaningful communication, and what's the point of starting something I can't finish? Besides, if last night's any indication, having a real conversation with Elizabeth will require approximately the same length of time it took Thomas Jefferson to write the Declaration of Independence.

Although it's unlikely Elizabeth can hear me from upstairs, I tiptoe back to the downstairs bath, shave with a ladies' pink plastic razor, nick my chin in two places, and then go into the laundry room, hoping to find a clean shirt that Kate hasn't already taken to my closet.

Alas, she's too efficient to leave anything undone, so I smooth the wrinkles in the one I've got on and hope nobody notices them underneath my sports coat. At least I always keep an extra in the hall closet. That comes from years of being called into emergencies while I'm having dinner or watching TV. A coat always reassures a patient that you know what you're doing, and having one in the downstairs closet shaves about four minutes off my response time.

I nab the coat, write Elizabeth a note and then head for the office.

It's a relief to walk in to the smell of freshly perked coffee and the sight of Lucille sitting at the reception-ist's desk with her hair in a bun.

"Good morning, Dr. Martin," she says, and I feel myself relaxing into something resembling normal.

"Good morning, Lucille. I want you to look up the number of an interior decorator and ask him to go over to my house today. I want the works. A complete overhaul. Tell him the sky's the limit."

There now. I've made Elizabeth happy and I can check *change house* off my list.

"Anybody in particular, Dr. Martin?"

"No. Just somebody with conservative tastes and a good reputation. Oh, and somebody who doesn't use purple."

Feeling a sense of accomplishment, I pour myself a bracing cup of coffee and go inside to wait for my first patient.

On second thought I go back to the doorway and clear my throat so Lucille will look up.

"Lucille, would you say I've been a good husband?"

I know this sounds like a foolish question to ask my receptionist, but Lucille is the one who wraps my gifts to my wife and books the trips we take. She's the one who knows about the times I've cancelled appointments so I could attend to some crisis Elizabeth had.

"Why, of course, you are, Dr. Martin. Any woman married to you could thank her lucky stars."

It's pathetic to need vindication from Lucille, but when you feel lower than the ugliest toad on the bottom of the scum pond, you'll do about anything to make yourself feel better. It's human nature. And now I feel like a better man, a man who will be able to figure out a wife he thought he already knew.

CHAPTER 13

"If marriage were hair, I'd perk it up with some
titian red."

—Beth

Jane wraps me in a bear hug, tells me I look great
and then ushers me into her sunroom and plies me
with food.

Her Southern pecan sticky buns are fresh from the
oven and the coffee is French roast. Sitting on a yellow
chintz chair, I try to settle back into my skin. About
the time Aunt Bonnie Kathleen died, I jumped out of
it and haven't been able to find my way back. I feel
like a woman trying to put on a Lycra leotard, hopping
on one foot while one leg of the leotard sags to my
knees and the other flaps around, whacking me in the
butt.

The note I found on the hall table this morning lies
on the coffee table between us. *Elizabeth*, it reads. *I'm*

sorry about last night. Could you pick up the pants Kate dropped off at the cleaners? Howard

When I hand it to Jane, she reads without comment. This is her way. She never offers opinions unless I ask, and then she won't venture one unless she knows the facts.

I tell her about the way Howard and I suffered through an evening together as if we were perfect strangers, and the way he fell asleep in his chair.

"So..." I add. "What do you think?"

"I think he's just being a man. Not many of them shine in the romance department. Even my Jim."

"I ran away, for Pete's sake. Doesn't he get it? Doesn't he see that I want to be more to him than chief cook, bottle washer and errand boy?"

"It's going to take more than one evening to settle your marital issues."

"But you think they can be settled?"

"Yes, if that's what both of you want." She studies me over the rim of her coffee cup. "Is that what you want, Beth? To make your marriage with Howard work?"

"That's the sixty-four thousand dollar question." Stalling, I reach for another bun and eat the pecans off the top. "This is going to sound awful, Jane. But I'm not sure what I want. Howard's a good man, a good father, a good provider, and a part of me wants to just settle down and say, 'Okay, so maybe it's not like it was when we were twenty years younger, but at least I have this.'"

I sip my coffee and nibble some more while she waits in that perfect patience I've come to depend on.

"But there's a little rebel inside me who's stamping her foot and demanding more."

"More of what, Beth?"

"Everything. Marriage, career, me. I want to be more. I'm tired of this mousy, careerless woman who sits at home waiting to be provided for."

"You're talented, Beth. Not every woman can compose a symphony."

"Neither can I." My voice cracks a little when I tell her about playing my awful opus for the Prices, and she reaches over to squeeze my hand. "I've wasted all these years chasing a bogus rainbow."

"It's not like you to give up."

"Who said I'm giving up? I'm just shifting gears, that's all."

Thinking about the changes I've made and all the ones I want to make, I'm suddenly seized by inspiration.

"I want you to cut my hair, Jane. And dye it red."

"I haven't done hair since college." She put herself through school working in an on-campus salon. "What if it comes out looking like a buzzard's butt?"

"Then it will be an improvement."

Our project requires a whirlwind trip to Walgreen's for Lady Clairol, then lots of towels, sticky buns and giggling. By lunchtime I'm viewing the results in the mirror—a flaming red pixie cut that suits my face as well as my newly acquired image, Elizabeth Holt Martin, a woman going places.

Now, if only I can decide which direction to go...

"You look ten years younger," Jane says.

"Do you think Howard will like it?"

"He's crazy if he doesn't."

The changes I've made so far are all cosmetic, but as I walk across the stretch of lawn that divides our houses, I feel a surge of hope. If I can change the externals, surely I can change the internals, the things that really matter.

I'm trying to decide whether to call Kate or just go over, when the doorbell rings. Standing on my front steps is a dowdy woman with ugly brown shoes and a starched hairdo that looks as if it wouldn't move in fifty-mile-an-hour winds. She introduces herself as Letitia Johnson from Beautiful Home Designs.

"I'm here to redecorate," she says.

"I'm sorry. You must have the wrong house."

She consults her notes and the brass numbers beside my front door, then nods and gives a self-satisfied smile.

"Didn't Dr. Martin tell you? He wants me to redo your entire house."

This is exactly the kind of thing Howard would do—hire somebody else to fix whatever he thinks is wrong. Why can't he get personally involved in our lives?

"I'm sorry you've wasted your time, but I don't need your services."

"Oh, but you haven't seen my swatches. Dr. Martin's receptionist said he wanted *conservative*, and I thought something in a nice scheme of blue and beige."

I swing open the door and she sees the long expanse of hallway leading into the great room.

"Oh…well, we could change that blue to green and perhaps warm up the beige a bit, and with new cushions and draperies everything would be just like new."

"No, it would be just like the old, except with a fresh coat of paint."

"Pardon?"

"I'm sorry. None of this is your fault. I've changed

my mind about decorating, but I'm sure Howard will pay you for your time."

As Letitia heads down my sidewalk with her boring color schemes and bland ideas, I feel as if I'm caught up in the same old song and dance, a marriage that keeps spinning around to a tune that never changes. If I want something, Howard pulls out his checkbook and buys it. If he wants something, he never says and I never ask. We're moving on automatic, keeping time to the same "Skater's Waltz" when we ought to be jiving and rocking to "Jukebox Saturday Night."

There was a time once—so long ago I hardly remember—when we talked of buying a small yacht and sailing around the world, taking a year off from everything and letting the wind take us to exotic adventures in faraway places. If we wanted to stop a spell in, say, Australia, we'd find temporary work and live like the natives. Then we'd sail away, revitalized, alive in ways we never could be if we'd remained in one place, landlocked and fearful.

We never did sail away. We never took a cruise. We never even took a detour.

Once when the girls were small and we'd driven to Disney World in Orlando, I suggested we come back through Atlanta and tour Six Flags, but Howard said we'd better stick to our plan, that he had the map already marked.

Last Christmas in a last-ditch effort for adventure, I got a brochure that featured a luxury cruise to the Bahamas, but Howard said he was too busy, and that I'd get homesick for Bonnie if I stayed away two weeks.

Well, I've proved him wrong. Sure, I got a little homesick while I was in Florida, but I didn't scuttle home in a weeping heap. I carried on.

Isn't that something to be proud of? Isn't it proof that I have the courage to turn over a new leaf? The only problem is, I don't know which leaf to turn over.

All this soul-searching is giving me a headache. I go into the bathroom to get a cold cloth and almost jump out of my skin. The redhead staring back at me looks like somebody I don't even know, a feisty woman ready to take on the world.

I turn this way and that, fluffing my hair and feeling a redhead's piss and vinegar flowing through my veins. Suddenly, I'm racing toward my car. Of course, I don't have to call ahead to visit my own daughter. I hardly ever do. Why should I start now?

By the time I've parked the car, Kate's already on the front porch. A good sign, I think.

"Goodness gracious…Mom…" She hangs back

like a shy child afraid to ask for cookies. "What have you done to yourself?"

"This is the new me."

"There was nothing wrong with the old you."

"You think not?"

She's hanging on to the doorknob and I'm clinging to the porch railing, both of us trying to figure out how to navigate the distance that separates us. Finally she swings the front door open.

"Come on in. Bonnie's napping, but I'll pour us some tea and we can talk."

She precedes me, plucking Bonnie's stuffed bear off the sofa, plumping the cushions that don't need it, straightening a stack of magazines that are already perfect.

"You'll have to excuse the mess. I haven't had time to dust and vacuum today. I've been making cupcakes for Rick's office staff."

"Why?"

"What do you mean, *why?*"

"A big law firm like that surely has a budget for snacks."

"Rick likes to take homemade. They're much better."

"Then why doesn't he spend some time with you

and Bonnie making cookies and cupcakes instead of
going off to golf every single Sunday afternoon?"

Instead of answering she vanishes into the kitchen
and returns with two china cups of perfectly brewed
hot tea served with silver spoons and real cloth nap-
kins.

"I mean it, Kate. I don't want to see you making
the same mistakes I did."

She sips her tea and then sets it on the coffee table
and races off to get a sponge where it sloshed over. I've
never seen her this nervous, this uncertain.

Leaving my chair I take the sponge before giving
her hand a quick squeeze.

"Kate, quit fooling with that housekeeping shit
and sit down."

"Mother!"

"I mean it. I've spent all my life trying to shape
myself into the square box I was in, and it breaks my
heart to see you doing the same thing."

She sinks into the sofa cushions, suddenly so bone-
less she looks as if she's disappearing into the plaid.

"I always thought you were perfect. I wanted to be
just like you."

Now I'm the one shocked into silence. All those
years wasted, I think. All those times I thought How-

ard was her hero, Kate was watching me, planning how she would imitate me.

But she used the past tense, so obviously I'm no longer perfect in her eyes. I have to make her see the truth.

"Kate, I was never perfect. I was just an ordinary woman coping. I left to change the landscape."

"Well, Florida is certainly that."

"I meant the internal landscape."

"Couldn't you have talked it over with Daddy first? That's what I would do with Rick."

"Maybe I was wrong about that. But he was so busy I thought he didn't care."

"You think he didn't? Why, he nearly cried sometimes when he talked about you."

Howard? Crying? I'm disturbed, exhilarated and dumbfounded. I've always thought of Howard as too detached to show messy emotions. But the news that I can move him to tears proves a level of passion I never dreamed he possessed.

"Thank you, honey."

"For what?"

"You've given me hope." Sipping my tea, I watch Kate's keen mind process this information. "Everybody needs hope, but sometimes we have to make brave and scary choices to make wonderful things happen."

I get up and hug her, really hug her.

"Please think about what I said, Kate."

Going down the steps I realize I didn't say everything I needed to or should have. Rick is only the tip of the iceberg. The real heart of the matter lies in all those childhood years when I stood back and let Howard take over Kate's upbringing, and maybe that's why she merely went through the motions when she hugged me back.

The car has been sitting in the sun, and everything is too hot to touch—a metaphor for my life. The list of hands-off things ranges from sex to past mistakes.

"It'll take time, that's all," I tell myself, and then I head toward Emmaline's store, Delicious Designs & More, and the two of us spend a giddy hour imagining the varying shades of purple on my bedroom wall.

"Good God!"

Howard's disbelieving tone nearly topples me from the ladder.

"I didn't hear you come in."

Obviously shock has rendered him speechless,

because Howard just stands there glancing from my hair to the bedroom walls and back.

"What have you done?"

He sounds just like Kate, and it strikes me that I didn't try hard enough with my older daughter, that I sat back in a newly married stupor and squelched my wild impulses while Howard turned her into the only three-year-old spinster on the block.

"You said you didn't want purple, so I got American Beauty Rose."

"I thought the interior decorator was coming."

"I sent her screaming back to the little square gray box she came from."

His shoulders sag, and all of a sudden I realize that Howard and I don't have a thing in common anymore. Maybe we never did. Maybe his early gallantry made me believe that he was my knight in shining armor and that I was the kind of woman who would always need rescuing.

"You didn't say a thing about my new hairdo." I run my fingers through it, purposely forcing the top into outrageous spikes.

"I liked it the old way."

"That's part of our trouble, Howard. You like everything the old way."

We stare at each other across a wrecked bedroom. Was it mere coincidence that I started painting here, or was it an unconscious desire to make this room uninhabitable, unable to accommodate two people who can no longer find their way across the bed?

There are a number of things I could say to end this impasse—*How was your day? Do you want a drink?*—but I don't. The ball's in Howard's court, and I'm waiting for his next move. Will he go for the goal this time?

"What's for dinner?"

I'm so sick of that question I could croak. I've heard it a million times, two million, three. It seems to be the overriding question in my marriage.

Instead of dignifying it with an answer, I climb back onto the ladder and swab vibrant paths of color across the drab walls while Pavarotti croons *"Che gelida manina,"* from Puccini's *La Boheme*. I wish I'd turned the volume up loud enough to rattle the china. I wish I had it loud enough to create a seismic disturbance. I wish anything except to be here in the disquiet of this room with Howard staring at my back.

The ringing of the phone slices the silence, and I pause with my roller brush in the air while Howard says, "Hello."

Then, "Slow down, Jenny. Are you okay?"

I'm off the ladder, across the room and jerking up the extension in the bathroom. The connection is filled with static, but I can hear enough to know that she's more than okay; she's excited.

"Fine," she says. "In fact, I couldn't be better."

"Hey, baby," I tell her.

"Mom! When did you get home?"

Years ago. Decades ago. In fact, I never left.

"Yesterday," I tell her.

"Great, Mom. Then you can pack some of my things and send them to me."

"What are you talking about?" Howard says.

"I'm staying in Sedona, Daddy. With Dean and his aunt Angel. She has the neatest house. It's on the side of these beautiful red cliffs overlooking the city, and I've got this great job as a waitress."

"You'll do nothing of the kind, young lady," Howard snaps.

"But, Daddy…"

"You'll get on the next bus and come home."

"Howard, let's hear what Jenny has to say first."

"You stay out of this, Elizabeth. She wouldn't be out there in the first place if you hadn't taken her side."

"This is not about taking sides. It's about Jenny's future."

"What kind of future does she have shacking up with that Clark boy?"

"Good grief," Jenny says. "I'm out of here."

"No," I yell. "Wait."

But my daughter is already off the phone. I storm out of the bathroom so mad I want to turn the paint bucket over Howard's head.

"Now see what you've done," I say. "She's just trying out her wings."

"It's not her wings I'm worried about. Tomorrow after lunch, I'm heading west to bring her home."

"Not without me, you won't"

"Fine. If you want to come, you can. But I'm warning you, Elizabeth. She's coming home to attend school in the fall, and that's that."

He marches toward the door, but wheels around for one last directive.

"We'll leave after lunch. I'll keep my morning appointments and have Lucille reschedule the rest. Before you pack, make sure my blue shirt and my shorts are clean."

I shoot him the finger behind his back, and then slam and lock the door.

"We'll just see about all that," I mutter, rummaging around the paint paraphernalia till I find my cell phone. After I punch in the number, it rings and rings, but Jenny never answers.

Who can blame her?

I'm going to kill Howard.

CHAPTER 14

"If it's raining, why don't I have an umbrella?"
—Kate

Here I am with dinner on the table, candles lit, one cupcake by each plate, the rest on a paper platter under plastic wrap, and not a sign of Rick. Not even a phone call. The clock's inching toward seven and he said he'd be home at six.

I fed Bonnie at five-thirty and if I don't get started with her bath and bedtime story, it will be nine o'clock before I get her into bed and she'll be cranky all day tomorrow.

"Come on, punkin'. Bath time."

The way my luck's running Rick will come home when I'm up to my elbows in Big Bird bubble bath and I'll look like something the cat left over.

I hate schedules that go awry and plans that don't pan out. It leaves me feeling as if I've been caught with my thumb up my nose and my brain at half-mast.

That's exactly the way I felt today with Mom's un-expected visit. Not that I wasn't glad to see her. I always am. Still, I didn't expect her to dig around in my marriage and unearth discontent.

And I certainly didn't expect confessions of inadequacy from her.

It's my vision of Mom as the perfect wife and mother that has kept me content to stay home and take care of Bonnie and Rick instead of doing something to satisfy my creative urges. To be honest, though, Mom's not the entire reason. I love Rick and want the same thing every woman dreams of: a happy home and a loving partner who makes everything else in life seem worthwhile.

Today Mom shattered any lingering illusions of herself as the role model of marital contentment. All those years I strived to get the attention of this goddess of home and family, all those years I viewed her as an icon of perfection just beyond my reach…gone. Wiped out in a searing moment of truth.

Now I'm kneeling in a puddle of sloshed-out bath-water, wishing I could shut my eyes and wake up to discover spring was just starting and Mom had never left.

She called change scary, and it is. I don't want to be scared. I just want things to be the way they used to be.

I want my heroes back. I want Mom planning the Fourth of July picnic and I want Rick whistling through the house, saying, "I'm home."

If he was going to be late for dinner, why didn't he call? And if he's in the middle of a big meeting, why didn't he have his secretary call?

It's common courtesy. Especially to a wife.

Make that a very wet wife because Bonnie decided to a dive into the bathwater and be a dancing mermaid, and now I have bubbles dripping off my hair and into my eyes.

"Okay, Bonnie. Enough of that. Settle down."

I'm reaching blindly for the towel when the phone rings. Well, let it. Only a complete fool would leave a three-year-old in the tub to answer the phone, even if it's the president of the United States on the line.

While I'm bundling Bonnie in a towel, Rick's voice comes over the answering machine.

"Sorry I missed dinner. Something important came up."

More important than a wife?

"I'll be working until about nine. Keep my dinner warm."

What about me? Don't I rate higher than roast beef?

"Oh, and don't forget the cupcakes. Everybody's looking forward to them. They know what a great cook my wife is."

Is that what my greatest achievement of the day is? A plateful of really good cupcakes?

A line from Mom's letter to Dad plays through my mind: *I don't want the most important thing I do all day to be making sure the toilet paper rolls out because that's the way you like it.*

Still thinking about her letter, I put Bonnie to bed, then go into the kitchen and eat roast beef, the fat already congealing on the top. I'm getting up to put Rick's in the warmer when a thought sinks me to my chair. Why did I eat mine cold? Why didn't I warm up my own supper?

Even worse, am I going to end up like Mom thirty years from now? Feeling like somebody who has been standing in a cold rain for a very long time?

I get up and put the leftovers in the refrigerator. Let Mr. Last-Minute-Call Rick heat his own dinner. If he doesn't like it, he can put on his big boy britches and deal with it.

On the way out the door I notice the cupcakes under wrap. My day's shining achievement. My claim to barefoot-and-pregnant-in-the-kitchen fame. Jerking up the platter I head to the garbage can.

But…wait. This moment feels big, worthy of ritual.

I toss them on the floor one by one and stamp on them, then I leave the *TAKE THAT!* mess and march upstairs to wash the blue icing off my feet.

CHAPTER 15

> "If logic were motor oil,
> she'd be three quarts low."
> —Howard

Gritty-eyed and pensive, I stroll into my office after another all-nighter on the sofa, wearing the same blue shirt I've worn for three days. If it weren't for the Old Spice deodorant in the downstairs bathroom, I'd probably stink.

Of course, I'm hoping once again that the jacket covers most of the wrinkles and that Lucille won't notice, but who knows what a sharp-eyed receptionist of twenty years sees?

"Good morning, Dr. Martin." She's as cheerful as ever, but she gives me a funny look as if to say, *Well, look what the cat dragged in.* She's probably thinking I've shacked up with some loose floozy instead of trying to find a comfortable spot on my own lumpy sofa.

Paranoia is new to me. As soon as I get something into my stomach maybe I'll be back to my old way of thinking. A man who knows what he stands for and never wavers. A man with the loyalty of a secretary who would just as soon jump off the Empire State Building as believe her boss would cheat on his wife.

A man who takes care of his family, for Pete's sake. How could Elizabeth think I'd let Jenny spend the rest of her days waiting on tables and living off the charity of others? What do we know about this relative of the Clark boys, anyhow? Nobody with a name like Angel can be taken seriously. It sounds like some made-up, hippie nickname.

"Are there any doughnuts in the break room, Lucille?"

"Two kinds. Cream-filled and plain. Which do you want?"

"One of each. No…make that two of each."

I had a piece of cold pie for dinner and another one for breakfast, eating both of them straight from the dish while standing in front of the refrigerator in my sock feet, wondering what Elizabeth was doing, worrying that she was painting the bathroom pink, too.

Great-granny's ghost! My wife has gone mad. What happened to the comfortable, solid marriage I thought I had? What happened to my nice, easygoing wife who fixed dinner every evening and darned my socks?

Not that I want her to be a drudge. Far from it. That's why I hired our housekeeper, Velma Lou. To make sure Elizabeth has the leisure time she needs to do whatever she likes.

But is she grateful? Is she happy? Oh, no. She has to chop off all her hair and dye it red. Like a baboon's butt.

My stomach growls in agreement.

"Dr. Martin?" With her eyebrows lifted into her bangs, Lucille looks as if she's about to take flight. "Are you all right?"

"I'm fine. Everything's fine. Bring the doughnuts into my office and then start rescheduling my appointments, starting with the one o'clock. You'll need to reschedule everything for the next week. Oh, and call Kate to look after Rufus."

Her mouth opens and then closes like a guppy's. She knows that nothing less than a major emergency could make me take a week off, but like the good receptionist she is, she doesn't say anything. Just nods and goes about her business.

Why can't Elizabeth be more like that?

Lucille brings in doughnuts, and I barely have time to scarf them down and wash the sugar off my chin before my first appointment arrives. Lord knows the state my poor digestive tract is in.

It's a relief to lean back and listen to Tootie Jo Hodges fantasize about smothering her mother with a goose-down pillow. She has a point. What mother in her right mind would hang a name like Tootie on a little girl, even if it was her mother's favorite sister's name?

At least Elizabeth was sensible about our children's names. Kate is named for Elizabeth's Aunt Bonnie Kathleen, a lovely, sensible woman, and Jenny is named for my granny Jennifer Martin, a prim-and-proper lady. Kate got all Aunt Bonnie Kathleen's fine qualities and more, but Jenny... Well, the name stuck, but unfortunately, the character didn't. Lord, Granny would never streak her hair orange and run off with riffraff.

I guess it's partly my fault. When Kate was a baby, I had more time to stay at home and participate in her upbringing. Not that Elizabeth's not a good mother; she is, but if she'd had her way Kate would have spent her formative years in overalls in the backyard making mud angels and searching for fairies. Or else running off to some flea-bitten circus to see elephants and dancing bears and grown men in women's underwear trying to keep from falling off a rope in the sky.

I made sure Kate had a proper upbringing with all the right educational books and toys and supervised outings to museums and art exhibits. And look how she turned out—a daughter to be proud of, steady, reliable, responsible and kind.

On the other hand, Jenny is a daily trial. A lovely girl, granted. Smart and funny and sweet when she wants to be, but Lord, when she was growing up, Elizabeth just let her go wild. Like that time Jenny got interested in frogs...

She was six when she developed an unhealthy interest in those ugly amphibians. I was sitting in my office making notes on a patient when I got a hysterical call from Kate telling me to come home, there were frogs all over her bedroom.

"Put your mother on," I said, and naturally I was expecting the same horror my teenage daughter had expressed, or at the very least, a grown-up reaction to the situation.

But no, Elizabeth was laughing her head off, telling me it was just one of Jenny's phases, and the best thing to do was let her learn about frogs in her own way and then she'd move on to something else.

"Like what?" I asked. "Cottonmouth moccasins? Elizabeth, I'm not about to sacrifice my older daughter on the altar of one of Jenny's whims."

I hurried home with the full intention of catching the frogs and turning them back into the wild, but have you ever tried to get a roomful of frogs to cooperate while two girls are screeching outside the door? I ended up dispatching the toads with the commode plunger and burying the whole mess out in the backyard. To hear Elizabeth and Jenny tell it, you'd think I had committed first-degree murder.

I should have put my foot down right then, but, of course, I was busy and thought Jenny would grow out of her foolishness. But look what has happened. I've got to drive all the way to Arizona to straighten out the mess Jenny has gotten herself into with those irresponsible Clark boys and a flighty aunt named Angel. Maybe I ought to take the commode plunger.

"Dr. Martin, do you think this means I'm going crazy?"

Tootie Jo's question jerks me back to my patient's obsession with wanting to do bodily harm to a mother who has been six feet under for two years. Ever since Elizabeth just up and left, I've felt the urge to commit a little mayhem, myself; so if Tootie is crazy, so am I.

"No, you're not. Take your pills, do your relaxation exercises and come back in two weeks."

After she leaves, I loosen my tie and breathe a sigh of relief. It will be good to go home early for a change. And who knows? Maybe the car trip with Elizabeth will be the best thing that ever happened to us.

I pack up my briefcase, say goodbye to Lucille and head home, cheerful, almost lighthearted. I enjoy being needed, and taking care of people's problems is my specialty. Once Elizabeth sees how well I handle Jenny, her regard for me will rise exponentially. We might even be able to sleep in the same bed again.

By the time I round the corner to my street, I'm whistling "Seventy-Six Trombones." Elizabeth will be over her snit, lunch will be on the table and my bags will be packed. If we move efficiently, we can be on the road by one-thirty.

I pull up in the yard and the trombones, the tambourines and the whole damned brass section die in my throat. Elizabeth is sitting in the front yard in a lawn chair. In her bathing suit! The new two-piece one that shows everybody on the block everything she's got. Her lips are as red as her god-awful new hair and her feet are in Jenny's old blow-up wading pool.

I screech to a halt and barrel out of the car...and that's when I spot my suitcase on the ground beside her, gaping open and empty as a black hole.

"Elizabeth? What in the world's going on?"

"What do you think, Howard?"

She stands up *real* slow, a sure-fire sign that she's got a snarling tiger in her tank.

"I'm doing your laundry."

Then as calm as you please she steps into the wading pool and starts stomping around. That's when I see my Fruit of the Looms floating around. Every last pair, from the looks of things.

On top of everything else, I'll have to stop and buy myself some clean shorts.

"Elizabeth...what the hell. Get out of there."

"Oh, okay. You can do your own packing." With this *excruciating* calm, she steps out of the pool and sashays toward the house. If anybody cared to stare out their window, they'd see my wife swinging her butt around like there was no tomorrow.

Mortified, I grab the beach towel draped across the back of her lawn chair and throw it over her shoulders.

"For God's sake, Elizabeth. What are you trying to do? Scandalize us in front of the neighbors?"

"If you worried about your own daughter as much as you worry about the neighbors, we wouldn't be in this mess."

I'm not fixing to have a private conversation in earshot of the neighbors, so I hustle her into the house.

"Now, would you care to illuminate me?"

"I'd like to illuminate you with a lightbulb straight up your wazoo."

"For God's sake, Elizabeth."

"Stop saying that. This is for Jenny's sake. Thanks to you, she didn't answer her phone until this morning."

"Did you tell her we were coming?"

"I did. But not to pack her up and haul her home like some misbehaving three-year-old."

"If she's going to act that way, then she'll be treated that way."

"Howard, don't you get it? She's not being childish, she's trying her wings. And if we clip them at every turn, we'll lose her. She'll become a statistic, one of those teenage runaways you see on the back of milk cartons."

Elizabeth's habit of overdramatizing used to amuse me, but now it just gives me ulcers. I feel as if I'm caught up in a crazy carnival ride, one of those Tilt-A-Whirls that spins you upside down till you get disoriented and can't tell where the ground is. Why can't we ease into old age like ordinary people?

"Elizabeth, I'm not about to let an eighteen-year-old child throw away her future. Now, are you going to Arizona with me, or do you want me to go alone?"

"If you think I'm going to let you go out west and provoke a showdown with my daughter, you're sadly mistaken, Howard Martin."

She jerks the towel off and flicks it at my butt. Hard.

"Besides," she adds, "I've got a thousand miles to make you change your mind about Jenny."

It's fifteen hundred, but Elizabeth never did know a thing about long-distance travel. The trip we took to Disney World when the kids were little is a case in point. We were down in south Alabama—Thomasville, to be exact—when Kate said, "Mom, where are we?"

"Why, honey...we're in the car!"

Of course, we all laughed and made a big joke of it, but all these years later I'm beginning to see that while I've always known where I was going—working hard to secure a good future for my family—Elizabeth has simply been along for the ride without the foggiest idea of where she's headed.

I guess I'm partially to blame. I've always indulged

her, let her drift along writing her music and taking care of the house and the girls.

Now, all of a sudden, she wants to take charge. And her without a clue. Good Lord, if I let her have her way in the current situation with Jenny, there's no telling where we'll all end up.

CHAPTER 16

"Could ninety-nine bottles of beer on the wall
save this road trip?"

—Beth

I used to picture us traveling along these roads, stopping to admire the Painted Desert and the Grand Canyon. Instead, Howard and I are barreling along, bleary-eyed and sore-tailed, not noticing a thing except the icy chill in this car.

I argued nonstop for Jenny's independence all the way to the Mississippi River bridge, but by the time we crossed into Arkansas I realized I might as well be talking to a stump. I swear, Howard is the most exasperating man I've ever met. How could I ever have thought he was sweet?

"She's eighteen, you know," I say in a final effort to get him to be reasonable. "Legally, she can do what she wants."

"Who gives a shit about legality if she's eating out of a garbage can?"

Good Lord. Is this my mild-mannered husband? Howard's never used profanities before.

"She'll have plenty to eat, Howard. No matter how much you bluff and bluster, I know you would never cut her off without a penny. Especially when she's done nothing wrong."

"This is not about right and wrong. It's about stupidity versus sensibility."

How like Howard to veer away from the real topic and try to turn this into a philosophical discussion. I have no intention of being drawn into that sticky flytrap. Instead, I unsnap my seat belt and lean into the backseat for a blanket.

"Great-granny's nightgown, Elizabeth. Buckle up. Do you want to get yourself killed?"

"Why, are you fixing to wrap this car around a tree?"

He mutters *shit* under his breath, which means I've won this round. If you call sitting hunched on the passenger's side of the car like a moody Buddha *winning*.

Now that I've stopped talking, I notice that Howard's relaxing. That won't do. If I want to win this battle for Jenny, I've got to keep him off balance, exhaust him to the point of submission.

And so I start humming "Ninety-Nine Bottles of Beer on the Wall." At first, he tries hard not to notice, but after forty miles of purposely tuneless humming, he's about to crawl out of his skin.

He swerves into a 7-Eleven so sharply I almost get whiplash.

"Gotta get gas," he mutters.

He's onto my ploy. Never mind. I'll just keep it up for another hundred miles or so, and then we'll see who wants to jerk Jenny up by the scruff of the neck as if she's some silly kitten who can't find her way to the milk saucer.

But first I need sustenance. Inside I load up with peanuts and chocolate bars and several sacks of corn chips. Not that they're my favorite. I prefer potato chips, but corn will make huge, crunchy sounds that will drive Howard even crazier.

We get underway again, and for the next fifty miles, I alternately hum and crunch, but the only thing I achieve is indigestion and an acute aversion to corn.

When did Howard and I come to this—warring parties always on the opposite side of an issue, especially if it involves the girls? I don't know. Maybe I'm the only one making war. I remember a time when we settled our differences with normal conversation in the civilized atmosphere of the living room.

Now we're racing through the night in a car filled with crumpled corn chip bags, chocolate smears and peanuts that went astray. I've worn myself out with antics designed to make him give in, and he's exhausted me with his dogged silence.

"Are we going to stop for the night?" It's long past midnight, and I want to know.

"That's the first sensible thing you've said since we left Tupelo."

"Does that mean yes or no?"

"If I can find a Comfort Inn, I'll stop."

Howard has an obsession about the Comfort Inn. I guess he thinks the name guarantees what it says. A highly unlikely prospect, considering the state of affairs between us.

Anyway, we pass a small Holiday Inn, a nice-looking Ramada and two no-name local motels, but he keeps on batting it. I'm not going to say another word. Even if he falls asleep at the wheel and runs us into a ditch.

Two can play this martyr game. Finally I see the Comfort Inn sign ahead, but I don't say anything. It would be like giving in. Let him think I'm indestructible, a woman who can scrunch into the corner of the car all night long and still remain strong and determined. Heck, even scintillating. Surreptitiously I reach into my purse and pull out a travel flacon of my favorite Jungle Gardenia perfume. There's nothing like fragrance to make a woman feel beautiful. Well, sex, but we won't even go there.

With my hands under the blanket, I spritz some perfume on my wrists, just on general principle.

"What's that I smell?" Howard says.

"I don't smell anything."

Let him think gardenia is my natural aroma. I'm certainly not primping for him.

"There it is." He wheels into the Comfort Inn— thank goodness—then gives one last whiff. "I could swear I smell flowers."

"Just get us a room and forget it."

He gets a room, all right, with two double beds. His and hers, obviously.

Not that I mind. In fact, I wouldn't sleep with him if he was the only man on Earth and I was in charge of single-handedly propagating the human race. For one thing, I'm too tired, and for another, I'm just plain mad.

While he's in the bathroom performing his nightly

ritual, I undress and chew some Tums, then crawl under the sheets and shut my eyes.

I hear the bathroom door creak open, then quietly shut, before Howard sneaks stealthily into the other bed.

"Well…good night, Elizabeth."

If I open my mouth for one word, even good night, I'll get on a roll again about Jenny and not be able to stop, so I don't say anything.

Maybe my attitude has to do with menopause. Along with PMS, it gets blamed for everything else, so why not this? Instead of explaining what's wrong I could just say, *Don't mind me, I'm menopausal.*

Jane says when hers started, she completely lost interest in sex. Since Howard obviously has, life would be simpler if that had happened to me; but *oh no*, I have to be the one in a million who gets a jolt to the libido.

"I know you're awake over there," he murmurs.

Clearly Howard's not done talking, but you can bet your bottom dollar he's not trying to start anything exciting, or even halfway interesting. I give a loud snore to prove him wrong.

"Tomorrow we'll get an early start," he adds.

Now I'm trapped. Since I'm pretending to be snoozing I can't ask, *How early?* Instead I squeeze my eyes shut and fall heavily into the blessed oblivion of sleep.

Howard wakes me up while it's still dark outside.

"We've got a thousand miles left to drive, Elizabeth, and I'd like to make it tonight."

In the motel's bad lighting his skin looks yellow, and the lank strands he tries to comb over his bald spot hang around his ears like silvery noodles. He looks like a grieving man who has suffered a horrible loss. And maybe he has.

Maybe we all lose things that are precious to us when we stop paying attention.

Look at Howard and me, enemies on opposite sides of the bed. We've lost us. We've lost sight of what's dear and wonderful in this life, this marriage, this family. We've lost fun and laughter and joy and conversation and respect and connection. But most of all, we've lost love.

Of course that could be fatigue talking, but still when I climb out of bed, full of loss and my own culpability, I'm carefully cheerful and helpful, determined to be the kind of helpmate a hurting man needs. Like that quintessential steel magnolia, Scarlett O'Hara, I tell myself *today is a new day*, and I decide to make it a good one. No more bickering in the car. No more guerilla tactics that give Howard a headache and me indigestion.

Oh Lord, I already have a stomachache. That's what I get from an overdose of junk food and too much introspection. Today I'm not going to think a single, soul-searching thought…except this: I ran all the way to Florida and all I changed was my weight and my hair. Howard came after me and all he changed (temporarily) was the clothing he wore. Externals. We thought by changing appearances, we could change everything.

How foolish. How shallow. Real transformation starts on the inside and slowly works its way to the surface. It's like making a pot of soup: the aroma wafts upward only after all the ingredients are mixed and stirred and simmered.

"I suppose if I suggest an Egg McMuffin, you're going to want a Hardee's sausage and biscuit," Howard says.

"Truce."

"You mean that?"

"Yes. I'm tired and grouchy and my stomach hurts. I don't want to fight. Actually, I never did, Howard. All I want is us to make sure Jenny's going to be okay, and then give her some space to grow up."

"Both of us grew up by the rules, and we turned out all right."

"No, we didn't, Howard. I'm fifty-three years old, and I don't have the least idea who I am."

"You're my wife and the girls' mother, that's who you are."

How can he dig around in other people's heads to extract the perfect truth and not have the slightest clue what goes on in his own family?

Remembering my resolution not to fight, I just sit still while he pulls into Hardee's (aha!) and orders breakfast at the drive-through window. While he's explaining how he wants two biscuits with sausage and eggs, jelly added, and one with only sausage, no jelly, I wonder what my life might have been like if I hadn't married Howard.

For one thing, I wouldn't be sitting bleary-eyed in a car trying to keep him from destroying our relationship with Jenny. Of course, I wouldn't have Jenny, or Kate, either, for that matter. Nor my precious Bonnie.

But I might have had other children. I might have married Jerry Luther, the high school quarterback who took me to the senior prom, and had his twin boys. He went on to play pro ball and he still has all his hair. True, his muscles don't look real. On the way home from the last class reunion, Howard asked me if I thought they were implants, and I said, "What in the world does it matter? He still has a wide-open smile and the kind of personality that naturally attracts people."

"Yeah, women," Howard muttered.

That's the only time I ever saw him jealous.

I picture myself as Mrs. Luther, sitting in a reserved seat at the Astrodome, cheering my husband as he makes his team's winning touchdown. Of course, Jerry's no longer playing ball. He's too old, but I know that he and his wife—his third, I think, and far too young for him—travel all the time. Perhaps if I were Mrs. Luther we'd be on our way to China, our good walking shoes packed so we could traipse along the Great Wall, admiring the exotic view.

Or I might not have married at all. If I hadn't met Howard, I might have continued my breaking-away-from-Aunt-Bonnie-Kathleen Bohemian ways and ended up in a loft in New York playing with the Philharmonic and writing lovely Pachelbel-like symphonies on my much-admired rooftop garden.

Thinking what might have been doesn't change what *is*. That's something I'm going to have to figure out, probably the hard way. Looking on the bright side, I have a thousand miles to Arizona and fifteen hundred back to decide what I'm going to do about my currently untenable situation.

CHAPTER 17

"Do I still know how to dance, even when
there's no music?"

—Beth

"Mom! You look great." Jenny races into my arms and then leans back to get a closer look. "Your hair's cool."

Jenny's own hair is streaked purple and blue and her skin is tanned the earthy color of the gigantic rocks that surround us. We're in the parking lot of a restaurant perched high atop rocky red bluffs near a vortex. Typically, she chose to meet us here instead of in our hotel room at the Comfort Inn.

Although Howard complained about her forcing us to drive another ten miles out of our way after driving fifteen hundred, he agreed because he knows she could have refused to see us altogether.

Jenny's a free spirit with a heart-connection to the

Earth, something Howard may never appreciate about his younger daughter. And truth to tell, this is partially my fault. As compensation for not having more to say about Kate's upbringing, I took over Jenny's and shut Howard out. No wonder he never bonded with her the way he did with Kate.

He gets a cooler greeting from her, an A-line hug that puts a polite distance between them. Afterward we say hello to the Clark boys and Jenny introduces us to their aunt Angel.

This is another of Jenny's clever ideas, bringing her support team, knowing full well that her father would never make a public scene. In the company of a virtual stranger, he's more likely to agree, however grudgingly, to her bold new plans for the future.

"It was nice of you to come all this way to check on Jenny," Angel Clark says, leaning across the table, openly friendly and smiling.

"We're her parents," Howard says, and I immediately try to smooth over his abrupt, almost-rude statement.

"What Howard means is that we want to make sure Jenny has everything she needs and that her staying with you won't be an inconvenience."

Howard kicks me under the table, but it's easy to ignore him because I'm fascinated by the woman he said probably grew pot in her backyard and hung out with criminal types. Maybe she does grow pot (I haven't seen her place yet), but I'm willing to bet she also grows culinary herbs and blooming cacti in a gracious garden next to a red-stone water feature.

She's the most beautiful woman I've ever seen, with eyes the color of the Mediterranean Sea and white hair pulled into a loose, curly knot on top of her head. In her flowing purple skirt and clunky silver-and-turquoise jewelry, she could be forty or seventy. It's impossible to tell because she's one of those ageless women with sculpted lips and cheekbones who make time irrelevant.

Angel. The name fits her.

"I'm looking forward to her company," Angel says. "Dean's, too. I haven't had young people in the house in quite some time."

I wish she hadn't plowed so quickly into the assumption that our daughter would be staying, because somewhere between the Mississippi River Bridge and Little Rock, Arkansas, Howard decided that "this Angel person obviously has some sexual issues because she's never been married and lives out in the desert with nothing but cacti and rattlesnakes to keep her company."

"Jenny won't be staying," Howard says. "She's going home with us."

"Daddy! How could you?"

Jenny bolts, and I race after her without even pausing to excuse myself. She's younger and faster in addition to being well rested, and by the time I clear the door I'm panting.

It's all I can do to croak, "Jenny, wait."

Luckily my daughter doesn't lump me in the enemy category along with Howard, because she backtracks and puts her hand on my arm.

"Mom, are you all right?"

"Let me catch my breath."

"Not here. I don't want to be around Daddy."

"He's just trying to do what he thinks is best, Jenny."

"Yeah. Best for him."

She leads me across the parking lot and up a rocky trail toward the top of a sky-saluting bluff, while I stumble along like somebody eighty-five instead of a woman with big plans and plenty of fire left in her belly.

By the time we get to the top, I have to sit down.

"Feel that, Mom?" Jenny spreads her arms and lifts her face to the soul-soothing blue of a sky that reaches forever. "Feel the energy? You can reach up and touch your dreams."

Oh, my heart hurts with joy. At least we did something right with our daughter.

"So, tell me about yours, Jenny girl."

She plops beside me on the sun-warmed rock, and we link our arms.

"Well, it's certainly not what Daddy thinks. I mean, there's nothing wrong with being a waitress. Some of the nicest people I've met on this trip are waitresses."

I've never been prouder of her. She picks up some twigs and starts making a small circle on the rocks— a little altar, I think, to the goddess of dreams.

"What I really want to do," she adds, "is be a photographer, and I thought I could stay here till I make enough money to buy a really great camera, and on my days off, I'd see what I could shoot. I mean... Mom...look at this place."

She stands up, dusts off her shorts and twirls around as if she's dancing. And I think she is. I think she's hearing music that no one else can hear.

"Isn't this the most spectacular scenery in the world?"

I try to see with my daughter's eyes, to look around

me and visualize possibility instead of loss, but all I can see are red bluffs and wide-open spaces.

My daughter continues dreaming and planning, twirling and talking about a famous photographer Aunt Angel knows. Jenny has the opportunity to learn from him, to find out if photography is really what she wants to do before she goes to college and we spend all that money.

All of a sudden I see my daughter's dreams rising out of the vortex-driven winds. I close my eyes and see my own, not as clearly defined, but still beginning to take shape.

Grabbing my hands, Jenny says, "Don't you see, Mom?"

"Yes. I see."

"I'm glad."

Jenny pulls me up, and we spin together on top of the world.

"You make me want to dance. Even when there is no music."

"You're amazing, Mom."

With sunlight and wind choreographing our movements, we twirl in wild abandon, sending forth dreams that spin into a net of hope.

"Elizabeth!" Howard's sharp reproof cuts through

our joy. "I'm trying to talk sense here, and all you can do is run off. Have you lost your mind?"

He's standing there scowling, his disapproval almost palpable. But this time, I will not compromise; I will not negotiate. There's too much at stake here, both for Jenny and for me. Indeed, for Kate and Bonnie and women everywhere.

"No, Howard. I'm just beginning to find it."

My wings unfurl, and without a backward glance, I jump into the net.

PART THREE

CHAPTER 18

"If my walls are purple is my soul singing?"
—Beth

I'm leaving you, Howard."

The wind is at my back and the dream-inspiring red cliffs of Sedona rise around me, giving me courage. There will be no running away for me this time, no fleeing without prior notice and with only a vague notion of what I want. This time I'm taking a stand.

While my husband stares at me dumbfounded, I say, "I won't let you drive Jenny away and ruin her life. She's staying here, and so am I until I'm absolutely certain everything's all right. Then I'm flying home, packing up my things and heading to Ocean Springs. And I'm taking the dog with me."

"Elizabeth, you're tired. We're all tired. You don't know what you're saying."

"I know exactly what I'm saying, Howard."

He looks as scared as I feel. Standing there running his hands through his thinning hair, Howard is the picture of frightened dejection.

"Are you saying you're leaving me permanently?"

"I'm going back to get my house in order, but I won't be returning unless there are some real changes. Not just in you, but in me, as well. If you can accept that, fine. If you can't, go ahead and do what you have to do."

In a last desperate move Howard goes to our daughter and puts his arm around her.

"Come home with us, Jenny. I know I can act like an overbearing ass…"

"Daddy!"

"I've heard you call me that, Jenny. And I admit it. Sometimes it's true."

I'm surprised and moved and even a little bit proud of Howard. But, still, I'm not fixing to change my mind. If I don't take this one last stand, I'll not only lose myself but something strong and precious for my daughters, as well.

"Honey," Howard tells her, "all I want is for you to be safe and get your education and get a good start in the world."

Jenny looks toward me for support. "Whatever you want to do is fine with me," I say.

"I'm staying, Daddy."

* * *

Howard left Sedona that day, but I stayed a week longer getting to know Aunt Angel, my daughter's boss and new circle of friends and meeting the photographer who is going to mentor her. When I left I was satisfied that, instead of repeating the mistakes of Aunt Bonnie Kathleen—God rest her soul—instead of stifling my child with rules and tight reins, I'd given her a chance to fly.

And now I'm standing in my own kitchen with my packed bags upstairs while Howard slumps on the bar stool.

"You won't change your mind, Elizabeth?"

"No."

He crushes a paper napkin in his fist, unfolds it and refolds it, then stands up and says, "Then I'll bring your bags down."

"Thank you, Howard."

"Call me when you get there? Just to let me know you're safe."

I nod, and he trudges upstairs. I can't stand to prolong this goodbye. By the time he gets to the car with my bags I'm already behind the wheel with Rufus lying on the backseat on his traveling pad.

When Howard leans in the window I smell his aftershave and have to blink back tears.

"Drive carefully."

"I will."

"And…Beth…I'm not going to do anything in haste…not until you tell me it's…over."

This is the first time Howard has ever called me Beth. That combined with the catch in his voice undo me, and by the time I'm out of the driveway and out of sight, I'm crying. Change is more than hard: it's heart-wrenching.

The sunswept cottage by the sea welcomes me. Before I even unload the car I race to the beach with Rufus for a spirit-restoring walk. No warm-ups, no purposeful hurry, just a lovely stop-and-go meandering that lets Rufus sniff every sand dune and allows me to watch as the sun sets over the water.

Afterward I grab my overnight bag, and we go inside. I put Rufus's bed beside mine on the rug, and we settle down for the night, two old friends finding comfort in each other's company.

The first thing I do the next day is buy red fringed lampshades and buckets of bright paint, and then I wait for Jane's arrival. She's in Ocean Springs by two o'clock and in typical fashion, immediately helps me pack Aunt Bonnie Kathleen's clothes for Goodwill.

When we stop for a tea and chocolate break, I don't beat around the bush about what's on my mind.

"Maybe I was wimpy not to just go ahead and make a clean break."

"No, Beth. A thirty-year marriage is not so easily tossed aside. And besides, what's the hurry? Redo the house, sell it, rent it, whatever you want, but there's no need to make a hasty decision that will affect the rest of your life."

Aunt Bonnie Kathleen's plain, functional lamps topped by my sassy new shades are a metaphor for my life: I've only halfway emerged into the woman I want to be. I want to recapture joy, rediscover passion. Unless I feel and know those things, how can I give them?

With my best friend, of course, this is easy.

"Do you know why I love you?"

"Maybe," Jane says, "but a woman always likes to hear these things."

"Because you're always supportive and you always let me have the biggest half of the Hershey's bar." I savor a bite of chocolate with almonds before adding,

"Oh yeah, and you don't think my fringed red lamp shades are tacky."

"Maybe we can find the right kind of lamp to go with them. You know, one of those plastic legs with the black fishnet stockings?"

"Wouldn't Howard die if he saw my lamp shades?"

"Who's to say he won't?"

"After what I've put him through, I'll be lucky to get a Christmas card from him, let alone a visit."

"You never know. Sometimes men will surprise the heck out of you."

He did surprise me—once. It was on our first anniversary.

For months I'd talked about moving my old Wurlitzer spinet piano from Ocean Springs, but he always had some excuse: it would cost more to move it than the piano was worth, he was too busy, we didn't have room for it. He was right about that. We were living in a one-bedroom, one-bath house with a living room barely big enough for our sofa.

Finally I quit talking and resigned myself to making do with my inadequate, tinny-sounding keyboard in the corner of the bedroom.

Then one Friday afternoon I came home from a long, exhausting band practice (I was getting my band ready for competition) to find the sofa and the coffee table missing. Panicked, I called Howard.

"You've got to come home. Somebody's stolen our living room furniture."

"You mean the room's empty?"

"I just said that, Howard. What's wrong with you? We've been robbed. Should I call the police?"

"Don't panic. Don't call anybody. I'll see you in a little bit."

Slamming down the receiver on my unconcerned husband, I was fully prepared to disobey and call the law, but about that time a big moving van pulled into our driveway…delivering a baby grand piano.

Howard arrived shortly afterward and kissed me right in front of the movers.

"Happy anniversary, Elizabeth."

"Howard, I adore it! But where will we sit?"

"What does it matter as long as we have music?"

That was his one and only surprise, but it's still one of the most romantic gestures I've ever heard of.

I wonder if he and I will ever have romance again? Considering our recent history, it's highly unlikely. I'll probably end up having my baby grand shipped down from Tupelo to my cottage by the sea. It's the only thing I regret leaving behind.

Besides Kate and Bonnie. And Jane, of course.

Now Jane says to me, "If you're not too tired from packing, let's get that purple paint and start painting."

"You got it, girlfriend."

I'm so filled with energy, I could jog to California and still have enough left over to march in the Rose Bowl Parade. It's excitement-fueled adrenaline, I guess. For the first time since that self-help seminar in Huntsville I see the wisdom of Glenda Wiggs's advice.

"Pri-ori-tize!" I yell, going for the paint rollers.

"Or-gan-ize!" Jane singsongs as she prances around the bedroom draping drop cloths over Aunt Bonnie Kathleen's functional furniture.

I'm going to change the furnishings, too. But first I'm going to bring this cottage to life with color—the purple of royalty, the yellow of the sun, the deep green of ferns hidden in cool forests, and the soft pink of romance. Who knows? If I decide to find one, I could meet a real hero down here.

"What color are these walls, anyway?" Jane asks as she applies the first swath of purple.

"Aunt Bonnie Kathleen used to call them olive, but I always called them turd brindle."

I stand back to admire the new, hopeful patch of purple across the top of the cloth-draped dresser. You can dream in a room this color. You can float out of yourself and land among the stars.

And then I remember lying on my twin bed in the small room down the hall, feeling the walls close in and wondering why my daddy never came for me. During those developmental years, the only thing that saved me from my dark thoughts was the sound of the surf.

I kept the window open year 'round so I could hear it. Even when Aunt Bonnie Kathleen caught me and warned I'd get pneumonia letting the winter winds in, I still cracked the window just enough to hear that connection with something bigger, vaster, more mysterious, more wonderful—and more dangerous—than the confines of my ugly walls and Aunt Bonnie Kathleen's rules.

Laying down my paint roller, I race around the room flinging open windows. One of them is stuck and Jane comes over to help me force it open.

"Listen to that," I say.

"I love the sound of waves."

"It's not just the sound of waves, it's the sound of hope."

* * *

Four hours later the room is purple and both of us are rummaging through Aunt Bonnie Kathleen's medicine cabinet for Ben-Gay.

"I know she has some," I say. "Every sane person over the age of fifty keeps at least one tube."

"Do you think one will be enough?"

"Heck, no, but I think there's some cheap Jack Daniel's in the kitchen."

"Now you're talking."

"That and a good cello sonata by Brahms will cure anything."

Along with the sound of the sea, the great thing about this cottage is that it has always been filled with music.

Hours later, lathered with Ben-Gay and mellow with Jack Daniel's, Jane and I fall asleep in the middle of a multicolored hooked rug in the future sunshine-yellow den while Brahms and the waves sing lullabies.

Jane leaves on Thursday.

"I hate to go before we've finished painting," she says.

We're holding on to each other in the sparkling yellow living room with her packed bags at our feet.

"It's not as if you won't be coming back. Besides…" I lean back to smile at her. "I have to have something to do after you've gone."

"Oh God, Beth…"

"Don't you dare cry. Listen, the next time you come down I'm going to throw a big party and invite the Prices and all my new friends."

"Knowing you, the house won't be able to hold us all."

"Good. We'll spill onto the beach and even into the surf. I'll have the party at night. We can all go barefoot and wear stars in our hair."

We give each other one last, tight squeeze, and then she climbs into her car and we wave until she's out of sight. I wrap my arms around myself, and decide to call Ken and Irma this evening to let them know I'm here. I'll invite them to dinner next week, knowing they'll come even though the drive is eighty miles. After all, what's eighty miles between friends? We'll sit on my front porch and listen to the music of the waves together.

The surf ruffles along the shore, and impulsively I kick off my shoes, whistle for Rufus, and the two of us romp along its cool, white edges. Then, suddenly, there is redemption: I hear music. Not just the music

of the sea, but blues coming from deep in my soul. First
the melody, haunting and insistent. Next the lyrics,
the gut-deep call and response that builds to the wailing lament of loss that can no longer be contained.

Forgetting my shoes, I race inside and sit at my old
spinet while music spills from my fingertips. With my
right foot on the sustain pedal and my left tapping the
rhythm, I start to croon.

"I got the low-down, lovesick blues… Oh, yes,
lord…I got the low-down lovesick blues…."

I rock from side to side, hitting the blues licks,
feeling the ache and pain of every bluesman born in
the Mississippi Delta, pouring out melancholy like
molasses on hot corn bread, swallowed up by loss and
yet still believing in salvation.

CHAPTER 19

"Am I the only normal person in this family?"
—Kate

I simply cannot believe this: Rick is still mad at me over the stomped-on cupcakes, Dad's walking around like the living dead, Jenny's strutting around out west, and Mom's still in Ocean Springs entertaining her friends and writing blues songs "like crazy." Her words. Not mine.

And what am I doing? Slaving over a hot stove fixing food for our annual Fourth of July picnic. For Daddy's sake—and Bonnie's—I'm trying to act as if everything is normal. But what's normal about half your family doing stuff that nobody else wants to acknowledge, let alone talk about?

The only thing Dad has said about Mom since she left is, "Why didn't she hire somebody to fix up Aunt Bonnie Kathleen's house?"

Poor Daddy. I understand how he feels. I wish I had a mother at home where she's always been and my daughter had a grandmother who would pop over and bake chocolate cookies and occasionally babysit. But I understand Mom's point of view, too. In fact, I'm beginning to feel exactly the way she did when she wrote that letter. Lost.

Rick's hardly ever home anymore. You could run a herd of elephants and three Mack trucks through all the time I have on my hands these days. I know he's working and that he wants to provide well for his family. Daddy taught me to appreciate a man like that.

But lately I've been thinking that I ought to do something more with my life. I'm beginning to feel like a half-finished woman, one of those drawings where the left side (wife, mother, daughter) is filled out in beautiful colors, but the right side is featureless and plain, no color whatsoever.

"Is that your mother's double-chocolate layer cake?"

I jump like somebody shot. Rick's home, and I didn't even hear him come in. Furthermore, it's only three o'clock and I'm not wearing a smidge of mascara and there's a chocolate stain on my pink shirt.

"You startled me, Rick."

"It smells good in here. Who's coming to the picnic besides family?"

"Nobody."

"Then what's the use fixing enough for an army? Why don't I just run to Finney's and pick up a pint of their potato salad?"

"We always have homemade."

That doesn't sit well with him, but I'm beyond caring. Of all days, why couldn't he stay at work and leave me in peace? I'm trying really hard here to make sure Daddy and Bonnie enjoy an ordinary family celebration.

But since he's here, I might as well take advantage of the situation and get a few things off my chest.

"I've been thinking lately that I need something else to do, Rick."

"Such as?"

Why do I feel like a witness on the stand instead of a wife?

"I thought I'd design a few children's clothes."

"I'm sure Bonnie would like that."

"Not just for Bonnie. For other people."

He stares at me as if I'm a specimen from outer space. Then in his careful lawyer's tone he says, "You're talking about selling them?"

"Yes. Maybe from the house at first, so I could be here with Bonnie, but later on I might get a little shop."

"I did not go to law school so my wife could be a shopgirl."

I can feel two big spots of heat rise on my cheeks, so I turn my back on him before I say or do something I'll regret. I'm not Daddy's girl for nothing. I know how to keep the peace when there are differing opinions in a marriage.

And lately there have been more than I care to think about. Or is it simply that they seem larger and more important because of Mom's stand? Is her bold restlessness rubbing off on me? If it is, maybe that's a very good thing.

Holding the stirring spoon as if it's a weapon, I face my husband.

"Listen, Rick, I don't want to do anything that will interfere with family life, but someday Bonnie's going to be grown and gone, and I'd like to have just a little something to keep me busy and give me a sense of accomplishment outside the home."

"Am I not enough?"

I slam the spoon into the bowl. "This is not about you. Can't you for once concede that somebody in this family has needs outside your own?"

He picks up the newspaper in this calm-before-the-storm way.

"I'm going onto the patio while you cool off. I don't intend to get into a fight with you before we go to your father's house."

"I'm not fighting, just trying to talk to you." He keeps on walking. "Dammit, Rick."

"See. That's just what I mean."

He eases the door shut behind him. Dripping chocolate across the kitchen floor and not caring, I walk over, open the door and slam it. Hard.

I don't care if I wake Bonnie up. I don't care if I wake up the whole world.

CHAPTER 20

"What do I want—enhanced attitude or
enhanced breasts?"

—Beth

Rufus is sleeping beside the stove, I'm cooking double-chocolate layer cake for my Fourth of July picnic and the radio is playing a rollicking version of "Ac-Cent-Tchu-Ate the Positive." It could be my theme song. I'm trying my best here, and that's really all anybody can do.

Johnny Mercer and Harold Arlen knew how to write music that resonated with the listener. I guess that's why I am constantly drawn back to blues and to music penned by such greats as Mercer and Arlen, and Kern, and those inimitable Gershwin brothers.

Humming along, I pop my cake into the oven just as the phone rings. It's Kate.

"Mom, do you have time to talk?"

"Always."

She tells me about her quarrel with Rick over her design plans, and my heart hurts for her.

"Is that why you never did anything with your music degree? Because Dad didn't want you to?"

"No, Kate. Your dad never tried to squash any of my career plans." A plus for Howard. I haven't thought about that in a long time. "That was all my own doing."

"Why?"

"It's a long story."

I sigh and she sighs, and suddenly I realize I'm repeating an old pattern, holding my past inside, showing a happy face to the world even when I was miserable.

"If you have time, I'll tell you," I say.

"Yes, please do."

I tell her about Aunt Bonnie Kathleen's *Father Knows Best* vision of marriage, and how my own fatherless state made me believe that a man on the premises was all I needed for happiness and contentment.

"But that's not true, Kate, and I don't want you to ever settle for less than what you want simply because somebody else says you should. I don't care if it's a husband, a parent, a teacher…I don't care who tells you to settle. Don't!"

"It's going to be an uphill battle with Rick."

"You know where to find reinforcements. I'm proud of you, Kate."

"Thanks, Mom. What are you doing for the Fourth?"

"The Prices are coming over, and I've invited their grandson, Adam, too. He actually lives here in Ocean Springs and usually fixes hot dogs for them."

We wish each other a happy Fourth, and no sooner do I hang up the phone than it rings again. It's Jenny saying that she and Dean and Aunt Angel are going to celebrate the Fourth.

"You and Dean seem to be having a good time out there. Are you two becoming more than friends?"

"Mom!"

"He's a nice boy. Both the Clark boys are. I was just thinking that something might develop since you're both in the same house."

"He's gay. Didn't you and Daddy know?"

How could we? People of my generation who aren't in professions that put us in contact with today's young people simply aren't attuned to those things.

"Mom? Are you still there? You're not fixing to get all phobic on me, are you?"

"Of course not. Keep on having a great time. And don't tell your father."

How awful is that? To advise my own child to keep secrets from Howard. He deals with the human condition in all its manifestations every day. Why shouldn't he be as compassionate and broad-minded as I like to think I am?

This kind of thinking just goes to show how far apart we've drifted. In the early days of our marriage I trusted everything to Howard, knowing that whatever I said or did, I'd have an understanding audience.

Wouldn't it be great if somebody would invent a time machine and we could all travel back to those periods in our life when everything was perfect? Or so we believed.

"I don't tell Daddy anything. When he calls he asks, 'How are you?' and I say, 'Fine, how are you?' and he says, 'Okay.'"

"Jenny, in spite of what you might think, your father loves you. I want you to remember that and try harder."

"Well, then why doesn't he?"

"Sometimes old people have a hard time bending, but young people are more resilient. Promise me you'll try."

She says she will, and when I finally get back to my meal preparations I think about Howard.

What is he doing right now? Is he wishing he'd

done things differently with Jenny? Is he missing her? Missing me? Wishing I'd come home?

This is a holiday made for sitting on a quilt under a live oak tree holding hands and watching the rainbow-shimmer of fireworks over the water.

Of course, I'm alone by choice, but still the ache is there. I can remember the Independence Days of my childhood, watching the distant play of fireworks across the water and wondering where my daddy was and why he left. The feeling of abandonment was so strong, I developed a dogged determination to never be abandoned again.

Now, of course, I won't be because there's nobody left to abandon me. I've made sure of that.

This flash of insight catches me high under the breastbone, and I stop in the middle of the kitchen floor. I feel like one of those cartoon characters the animator propelled off the cliff and then left hanging in midair.

The phone rings again. It's Jane.

"Are you doing okay, kiddo?" she says. "With the holiday coming up and all?"

"Great."

Why unload an unsettling insight on my friend? She's doing enough for me already without having to play psychiatrist, too. Of course, if I really need a psychiatrist I don't have far to look. I'm married to one.

Or I was yesterday. Who knows? Maybe he's seen an attorney and divorce papers are in the mail even as I speak.

But I'm not going to dwell on that. Why should I? Howard and I don't need each other back the way we were; together we're toxic. We've already proved that.

"I'm getting ready for a party."

"It sounds like you're settling in, Beth. Are you?"

"I don't know, Jane. All I know is I'm involved in a massive makeover. Some women get face-lifts and breasts implants, but I'm giving my house the face-lift, and the only implant that interests me is a new attitude. I'm composing again, making friends and sleeping with my windows and my mind wide open."

"That's great."

She doesn't ask, *What are you going to do with the songs*, which is one of the reasons I want to tell her.

"I don't know if I'll ever do anything with my new songs, but it feels good just to have the music pouring out. And I think they're good, Jane."

I smell the cake and tell her to hang on a minute while I take it out of the oven.

"Enough about me. What's going on with you?"

"You're not going to believe this, but Jacob has broken his engagement. I hate to say it, but I'm glad."

"Shoot, Jane, say it. Nobody thought Miss Perfect Pink Nail Polish was right for him. He's too smart and wonderful."

"He is, isn't he? Oh, and Beth, he's going to Sedona next week for a medical conference. I told him to check on Jenny."

"Great. Listen, Jane, I don't ask Kate because I don't want to put her in the middle of my marital problems, but is she still playing nursemaid, house-keeper and cook to a man old enough to learn to wash his own clothes?"

"You haven't talked to Howard?"

"No. I demanded space and I guess he's giving it to me."

"I haven't seen Kate over there in the last few days. But I have seen delivery trucks from Paul's Pizzas and Chong Ye Chinese."

It might not seem much to most folks, but for Howard that's a giant step.

"Hello, I'm Adam," the Prices' grandson says.

Holy cow and root, toot, tootie with whipped cream and cherries. Who needs firecrackers to celebrate the

Fourth? Suddenly I'm Eve. Forget attitude adjustments. Shallow woman that I am, all I want is collagen lips, breast implants and a nice, flat liposuctioned belly.

"Welcome to my picnic," I tell him, and then I turn cartwheels to the kitchen.

Not really, of course. For one thing, his grandparents are looking and for another I'd fall flat on my butt. And, of course, I'm married.

Separated. Living apart. Not cohabitating with my husband.

There is no end to the excuses your little devil tempter will make when your weary angel lowers her guardian's wings. There is no end to rationalization when a woman who hasn't felt physically attractive to a man in a very long time suddenly has a man looking at her as if he thinks she's the sexiest thing since Bo Derek strutted herself as the perfect 10.

"Thank you for inviting me."

Adam, who smells like wind and surf and something good that should be eaten in small bites, follows me into the kitchen while I try to figure out his age. When Ken and Irma said *grandson,* I thought about a little boy in knee britches, which obviously is not *this* Adam who tops six feet by a delicious two inches.

Perfect height. Perfect everything, now that I see

him at close range in jeans and a T-shirt. Except age, of course. How old is he?

He's leaning against the cabinet and handing me something. What? I've been too distracted by my calculations to notice the bouquet in his hand. Math is no my strong suit, but *oh joy*, gardenias are.

These are lush and rich smelling, and when I get Aunt Bonnie Kathleen's cut-glass vase from the cabinet I feel like somebody who recently got crowned Queen of Last Chances.

But, is he a last chance? There's the matter of a marriage certificate and old age. Mine.

Of course, Adam could be close to forty because Ken and Irma must be in their late seventies or even eighties. Still, that's a huge age gap. I wonder how Adam feels about older women.

I'm not long finding out. When we take the food outside to the picnic table, he gallantly settles his grandparents on the shady side, and joins me in the sun on the other side, moving close enough that his upper arm occasionally brushes mine.

As if that weren't signal enough, he looks deep into my eyes when he talks to me about directing the high school band at Ocean Springs.

"I used to direct band," I say.

"She composes, too," Irma says. "Beth, you should play your symphony."

"I haven't told you yet because I wanted to make sure it's not a fluke, but I'm composing blues now."

"You'll have to play for us." Ken glances from me to his grandson. "Maybe Adam can accompany you. He always carries a harmonica in his pocket."

"I'd love that," Adam says.

He's looking directly into my eyes again. Later, after we've cleared the table and stowed the dishes in the washer, he leans against the piano with his hands cupped around a blues harp, coaxing out haunting riffs, key of G. They weave around my keyboard melodies and under my skin and into my throat until I can't say a word.

Irma says, "That was great."

"Fantastic," Ken agrees.

But Adam says everything. "Wonderful."

He covers my hand on the keyboard and I feel beautiful. I ask Irma to play, and when I leave the piano I'm conscious of my body, of the sway of my hips and the swimmer's tone of my legs and the way my T-shirt moves across my torso.

Irma plays Broadway tunes while we sing. Typical musician, Adam is the only one who knows all the

words and in my newly aroused state I think he's singing just for me. If he's not, I don't want to know. I
want to wallow in these luscious feelings.

They leave at the same time because Ken and Irma
are staying with Adam overnight to avoid a long drive
home in the dark.

I hug the senior Prices and promise to visit soon,
then smile at Adam. In my sexually charged state I'm
afraid I'd move in too close, hang on too long, look
like a foolish older woman flirting with a younger
man.

"I hope you can come again," I say.

"Oh, I can and I *will*."

CHAPTER 21

"Is Viagra enough?"

—Howard

I wish I had told Kate we wouldn't have our usual Independence Day picnic this year. It's not the same without Elizabeth. Nothing's the same.

Of course, Kate would have been disappointed because she loves tradition. Although it's nice to have the same potato salad and cake Elizabeth always made, seeing the food sitting there on the wrought-iron table only half-eaten makes me even more lonesome.

I should have invited the Meadors. Jane and Jim might have made this holiday more bearable. And of course, Jacob, too. I saw his car come in this morning.

It must be nice to know where all your children are. Ever since Elizabeth talked me into leaving Jenny in Sedona, I've felt as if she has simply disappeared from my life in the same way that her mother did.

"Come on, Daddy," Kate says. "It's time for fireworks."

I feel guilty because Bonnie's clapping and my daughter's expecting a show of enthusiasm from me or at the very least a spark of life, but all I can do is sit here on the glider hoping it will rain. Thunderclouds have been gathering since midmorning. They're heavily banked in the south now. I wonder if Elizabeth is getting wet.

"I'll do the fireworks," Rick says, and I'm so relieved I have to blink back tears.

"No, Rick. Daddy *always* does them."

"That's okay, Kate. I just want to sit here and enjoy the show this year."

Mosquitoes whine around my ears, and I slap at them while the bug zapper cracks and sizzles. I had planned to screen in the patio so we could enjoy the outdoors in summertime without the hassle of pesky bugs, but that was when Elizabeth was here to make entertaining fun. In fact, she made everything more fun.

I don't know what I'll do now. About the screens or anything else, for that matter. What's the use of planning home improvements if she's not around to share the results?

She used to love sitting in this glider watching the moon and the stars. She'd sit out here when the moon was full, then come inside and say, "Join me, Howard. It will take your breath away."

Sometimes I would, but more often than not I wouldn't. Maybe that's the basic difference between Elizabeth and me: she wants wonder, I want routine. Maybe if I had come out here more often to watch the moon she wouldn't be in Ocean Springs under the guise of redoing Bonnie Kathleen's house and I wouldn't be up here facing the prospect of a string of lonely holidays.

Over the years I've heard patients, especially the single ones, bemoan the loneliness of holidays. Of course I understood their pain, but purely in a clinical sense. Until today I could never empathize with their bone-deep sense of isolation.

Kate would be hurt if she knew how I felt, so I make myself clap when Rick shoots off a bottle rocket that lights up the sky with red, white and blue. How can she possibly understand this kind of lonesome, the kind that's even worse when you're surrounded by people?

I feel myself choking up again, so turn my head while I fumble around for my handkerchief, hoping nobody will see.

"Daddy?" Kate's hand is on my arm, and she's leaning over me as if I'm some senile old fart instead of a man in his prime. "Are you all right?"

"Of course, hon. I got a bug in my eye, that's all."

I'm so far from all right, it's a wonder I don't choke on the lie. As for being in my prime, that's another illusion. Recent events certainly contradict the idea, but I don't dwell on it. No use adding another burr to the pile that's pricking my saddle.

"I have a great idea, Daddy. Why don't you come over and spend the night with us?"

Kate's too smart to fool. She's just like me, gifted with the ability to see through the smoke screens people put up and get directly to the truth. Of course, I didn't see Elizabeth's truth, and now it's too late.

"I'll be fine here, hon."

"I mean that, Daddy. We'd love to have you."

Her offer is tempting—a night in a bed where the empty pillow on the other side doesn't remind me of Elizabeth. Kate has plenty of room for me. In fact, her house is large enough I could have private quarters that include my own bathroom.

I picture myself not only staying the night, but moving in. I could sell this house where every nook and cranny is filled with bittersweet memories and create a simpler life, one that involves nothing more complicated than getting up in the morning, going to work, being pleasant company at the dinner table and then going to bed at night.

Naturally I would bear my share of the expenses. I may be many things (not much of a stud, for instance), but a cheapskate is not one of them. Too, I'd be right on the premises when Kate needs someone to watch Bonnie. Think what she'd save on babysitting fees, alone.

"Kate, it's about bedtime for Bonnie."

Rick's reminder brings me to my senses. Moving in with them ranks as one of the worst ideas I've ever had. No house is big enough for two families, not in today's fast-paced, anxiety-producing society. And considering the cool distance between my daughter and her husband today, even staying overnight is a bad idea.

Did they think I wouldn't notice? Even in my current state of self-absorption I couldn't fail to see Rick's exaggerated politeness to Kate and her unusual sharpness to him. I'm not privy to what's going on between them—nor should I be—but I have no intention of getting in the middle.

"Rick, please don't interrupt. I'm trying to get Daddy to spend the night with us."

There she goes again, snapping his head off. My

son-in-law shows a quick flash of irritation, but to his credit, smoothes it over very quickly.

"Sure, hon. That would be great. We'd enjoy having you, Howard."

"Thanks, but I have a lot of work to catch up on. You two kids go on."

"We'll just leave the food with you," Kate says, but I tell her to take it. As much as I hate the thought of Chinese takeout or Kentucky Fried Chicken for one, I don't want any more reminders of this picnic.

Bonnie sidles up to me, and I lift her for a goodnight hug. "Sweet dreams, sweet pea."

She giggles and then says, "See 'ou 'ater, al'gator."

"After a while, crocodile."

It takes every bit of willpower I have to say this to my granddaughter. This is the exchange she always has with Elizabeth.

Will the time ever come when I can do all the things we used to do together and not think of her? I wish I knew how to get her back.

After they leave I go inside…and there sits Elizabeth's baby grand, untouched. In previous years, the whole family would gather in the living room, and she would sit down at the piano and play patriotic songs while the rest of us sang off-key.

Thank God Kate didn't suggest we sing this year. I'm as tradition-loving as anybody, but there's only so much tradition a man can take when he's lost his right arm.

Already I can tell this is going to be a Tylenol PM night. There's no use getting in bed and tangling myself up in the covers while my mind gnaws on the beat-up bone of my marriage.

I nab the bottle from the back of the medicine chest, and when I shut the door, I look myself in the mirror. Great-granny's ghost, I look like something that ought to be taken into the woods and shot. If being separated from Elizabeth can do this to me, imagine what being divorced would do. Probably kill me.

Maybe I'd better talk to Jack Warner before I fall apart completely.

It feels funny being on the wrong side of the psychiatrist's couch. Here I am stretched out like one of my own patients while Jack studies me in that Buddha-like way of his.

"Relax, Howard," he says.

"How can I? I know all the tricks."

"Forget doctor/patient protocol and just talk to me as a friend."

"Then why in the hell did you put me on this couch?"

"I've never heard you use that kind of language. When did you start? After Elizabeth left?"

"No, before, actually. But I don't give a rat's ass anymore about language. All I want to know is *what* did I do wrong?"

"You tell me."

"I don't know. Maybe I didn't pay her enough attention, but…good Lord, we've been married nearly thirty years. Wouldn't you think she'd want to stick it out? It's not as if we're spring chickens. Who would want us now?"

Jack doesn't say anything, which makes me squirm. I wonder if this is how my patients feel when I sit in my chair and wait for them to figure out the uncomfortable truths?

"Do you think she's having an affair, Jack?"

"Do you?"

"I don't think so, but she did dye her hair. Bright red, if that tells you anything."

"What does it tell you?"

"It looks like she dipped it in red icing and styled it with a kitchen mixer, but I guess I'm stodgy. I was used to her natural color."

I pat my own rapidly balding pate. Face it. Elizabeth looks pretty darned good now, and I'm no catch, even if you're not very picky.

"Then there's the matter of sex."

This is hard for me to say because I was brought up to believe that matters of intimacy were best kept within the bedroom walls. But since I'm here to get help I might as well bare it all, pardon the pun.

Jack has shifted so I can't see his face—a clever ploy. I've used it myself. Still, this feeling of speaking anonymously gives me the courage to carry on.

"The truth is, I'm experiencing a little…hmm… sexual dysfunction."

His silence gets on my nerves. Why doesn't he say something?

"It's probably just a passing thing," I add. "It could be prostate trouble…I had it once…about ten years ago."

It was only after I'd embarrassed myself three or four times in the bed that Elizabeth suggested I see Dr. Paulk.

"Maybe I'll see Dr. Paulk," I say.

"Ask about Viagra."

"What?"

"Viagra, Howard. It's fairly common for men our age to need it."

I should have thought of this sooner, but I *did* have that little flash of passion in Florida. Besides, every man likes to think of himself as invincible, a hero to his wife. Having to take a pill before you can meet her needs lets the air out of that ego-inflated balloon.

"Have the two of you talked?"

I'm glad Jack has left my floppy subject and moved on to something more substantial.

"Not lately."

"You should. If you have any hopes of reconciliation, the two of you have to communicate on a real level. You know that, Howard."

"Yes. I've told my patients that hundreds of times. But advice is easier to give than to take."

"Coming to me was a good start. It shows you're willing to work with Elizabeth toward a compromise that's satisfactory to both of you."

I thank Jack and head to my car. His advice sounds reasonable to me, but I don't picture Elizabeth getting too excited over a marriage that's a "satisfactory compromise." She's fanciful and romantic. I guess it's the artist in her.

They say opposites attract, which was certainly the case with Elizabeth and me, but the irony is that the differences that drew us together have become the source of our discontent. Take, for instance, the matter of Paris.

Elizabeth has wanted to go for years. She's built it up in her mind until you'd think the Eiffel Tower was some sort of sacred totem. Not that I have anything against Paris. It's just that I believe in paying attention to my business. That's what keeps a roof over our heads. If I flitted off on every one of Elizabeth's whims, my patients would find somebody else who kept dependable office hours.

A car horn blares and a red-faced driver shakes his fist at me.

Suddenly the stop sign on the corner of Robins and Jefferson springs out at me, and I slam on my brakes. Good Lord, if I don't do something about Elizabeth I'm fixing to be a traffic statistic.

That would serve her right.

The thing is, I don't want to serve her right. I want her back home in my bed where she belongs. Not just back in my bed: back in my life. She was the Fourth of July sparkler that put sizzle in my drab, ho-hum existence.

There's one major problem with reigniting my fizzled-out firecracker: I still don't have the faintest idea how to get her back. But I'm going to work on it. By George, I'm not letting her get away without a fight.

Pulling into the library's parking lot I scan through my cell phone's list and punch in Dr. Paulk's number.

CHAPTER 22

"Good grief, Dorothy, you're no longer
in Kansas."
—Kate

I love the smell of fabric stores, the look and feel of
the different types of cloth, the endless possibilities
presented by bolts stacked in businesslike fashion
along shelves that reach higher than my head. While
I'm browsing through batiste and endless varieties of
lace, Bonnie is sitting at my feet "reading" *The Velveteen Rabbit* upside down.

"See 'ou 'ater al'gator," she says, before turning the
page and running her finger along the lines, making
up words as she goes.

She's missing Mom and can't understand why
Nana can't pop over anymore. Maybe we'll take a
road trip to Ocean Springs. I'd love to talk to her in
person. I'd love to say, "Mom, you were right, after all."

She's just an ordinary woman coping. I guess we all are. The trick is not to settle. She has said that over and over—in her letter to Dad, in her phone conversations, in her actions.

Now I know exactly how Mom felt when she left—scared, exhilarated and *free*.

I hold up two swatches of fabric, one pale pink, the other blue.

"What do you think, Bonnie?"

"Can I hab it?"

"Later. I'm going to make a beautiful dress and I'll let you have the scraps."

She claps her dimpled little hands. "Goodie."

I wish I could please everybody that easily. Wait a minute. It's not my job to please everybody. That's how I lost myself in the first place.

A weight lifts from my shoulders as I head to the checkout counter. Afterward, I dial Dad to ask if he needs me to pick up anything while I'm in town.

"No, Kate. I'm fine. I picked up my cleaning on the way to work and I'll stop by Kentucky Fried Chicken on the way home."

He sounds much better than he did on the Fourth. Perkier, somehow, and that's a good thing. Now that he's not so needy, I can use my energies to carve out a new path for myself.

"Have you heard from Mom?"

"No. I'm giving her some time, Kate. And maybe I needed some, myself."

Back home again, I create a play corner for Bonnie in the sewing room and set to work, stopping only long enough to make sandwiches for lunch.

When I hear the front door open and Rick's footsteps going from the downstairs hall to the kitchen, I resist the knee-jerk urge to race downstairs.

"Kate?"

"Up here."

"I'm home."

"I know. Come up here."

There's this *big* silence, but I don't rush to the door and stick my head out. Let him be the one to wonder, for a change. Finally he plods up the stairs. I know that walk. It says, *I'm tired because I've spent all day earning the living. Everybody should pay attention to me and toe the line.*

Starting today, I'm blurring the lines.

Rick's in the doorway with his mouth hanging open. Normally this house is so orderly you could have a reception for Martha Stewart and not have to clean a thing. Now there are fabric scraps and bits of lace on the floor, my designs are spread all over the cutting table, and Bonnie is sitting astride the yardstick, pretending it's a horse.

"What's going on?" His voice is careful, controlled.

"I'm designing children's clothes." I hold up a partially finished dress. "My goal is to debut the Kate's for Kids designs at Celebration Village in October."

Rick's thunderstruck. Even the mention of his office's favorite charity doesn't move him.

Celebration Village is an annual fund-raising event for Hospice House featuring upscale merchandise displayed in festive booths. The timing and the venue feel right, and I like to think that my first act of business will benefit a good cause.

Finally Rick says, "You mean that, don't you?"

"I do. I'm not asking. I'm telling."

He stares at me across the room, no doubt seeing wreckage, while all I see is opportunity and growth.

"Is this a deal breaker, Kate?"

Am I ready to risk everything for my dream? Mom did, but nobody knows how that's going to turn out. Still, I have the electrifying sensation of a woman coming out of a coma.

"Yes," I say. "It's a deal breaker."

"All right, then." He's quiet for a while, and I don't

breathe. "I'll take you and Bonnie to dinner and we'll discuss ways we can make it work."

"Okay. Let me just change our clothes first."

"I'll wait downstairs."

When he turns to leave I expel a long breath. His footsteps going down tell a different story—compromise.

"That was victory, Bonnie." I pick up my daughter and give her a big hug. "Look and learn."

CHAPTER 23

"Lust strikes again."

—Beth

Is three days long enough to put out a bush fire? Pun absolutely intended.

Adam wanted to come over the day after my picnic but I said I had a few maintenance chores to take care of first—polishing my toenails, renewing my hair dye, mud packing my wrinkles, doing a hundred crunches a day. Maintenance is tougher after fifty.

I wish somebody would invent a mirror that leaves out the details and shows the stuff that really matters. If that were true, instead of being aghast at the vertical bulldozer tracks above my lips and the eye pouches big enough to pack and carry to Kansas, I would see compassion and kindness and spirituality.

Of course, in addition to being an older woman

worrying about how she looks to a younger man, I don't want to rush into anything. I know that sounds ridiculous from a woman who spent twenty years composing one symphony, but Adam is music of a different kind. He's the cha-cha, the rumba, the tango. Not the kind of dance you dabble with but the kind you plunge headlong into and then find yourself the center of attention on the dance floor.

Ocean Springs is a small town. People will talk. Word would get back home. Kate and Howard would do more than talk.

There's a lot at stake here.

Now Adam says, "I think we can make this work."

Well…for a minute I think he's reading my mind. But he's talking about the arrangement we're doing on "Lonesome Blues." We're sitting on my front porch with our shoes kicked off, scoring the song for his band while Rufus snoozes underneath the porch swing.

"I have a really strong trumpet section," he adds. "This song will be great for them."

"Oh, I'd love to hear it."

This is not a ploy. In the quiet of this cottage by the sea I've learned to move into stillness, to feel every emotion, to listen to my instincts, which is really listening to the universe whispering truth in my ear. One of those truths is that I was never more alive than when I worked with the junior high band.

"Summer band camp starts tomorrow. Why don't you come to the high school? Maybe you could give us a few pointers."

"That would be great."

We both reach for the music at the same time and our hands collide. Adam takes mine and I feel the stirrings of something lovely, of femininity and passion, not merely passion for life but a lusty, physical need that heats up my skin.

"Beth?"

The physical passion is too wonderful too soon. I jump up and smooth down my shorts.

"It's getting dark. Let me turn on the light."

I flood the porch with light and then sit down a deliberate distance from him. We're almost finished here. I could invite him to supper, but I'm afraid I don't have enough willpower to resist if he wants to do more than hold my hand.

And by George, I *will not* go from one safe harbor to the next. I moved quickly from the overprotective harbor of Aunt Bonnie Kathleen to the steady port of Howard. I'm determined not to jump onto the exciting dock of Adam Price without ever putting my feet in the water, let alone plunging in to see if I can swim without a life jacket.

"I should be going," he says.

If I stand he might try to kiss me, so I don't.

"I'll see you tomorrow."

The football field is exactly as I remember, the band spread out in precise formation, brass instruments gleaming in the sun, the air filled with the scent of youth and excitement and possibility.

Adam sees me and hurries over.

"I'm glad you came, Beth. I'm eager to try out 'Lonesome Blues.'"

"I'm nervous. This is like sending a child off for a first day at school."

"Don't worry. Everything's going to be all right."

Adam sounds like Howard. That has always been his constant reassurance to me, and as I sit on the sidelines and watch the band prepare to play my music, I wonder what my husband is doing now and whether he's sitting in the sunshine somewhere in Tupelo admiring the way a younger woman smiles at him.

This is not the fantasy of a jealous wife; it's a real

possibility. Howard may not look like George Cloo-
ney, but he has two things many women want: a pres-
tigious address and a big bank account.

Of all times to be thinking about Howard! The
band is warming up and I need to concentrate on
how my music sounds. This is a big moment for me,
hearing someone else perform my song.

Adam lifts his baton and the music gets underway.
This is the band's first time, and they're shaky. Still,
I feel the passion of the music, the haunting beauty,
the absolute *rightness* of this song.

"Did you like it?"

Adam's standing in front of me, and I'm still trans-
fixed, even though the band stopped playing a minute
ago. Emerging slowly, I look across the sea of young
faces and find nothing but smiles.

"Oh, Adam…" That's all I can say because tears are
streaming down my cheeks.

He touches one tear, then leaves to dismiss the
band for a fifteen-minute break. While the field emp-
ties of clamoring musicians, he strolls back and sits
beside me on the bench.

"That was really great, Beth. You have quite a gift."

I can only nod. With great gifts comes great joy…
and great responsibility. How am I going to use this

talent? Certainly not by putting the blues songs on the closet shelf for twenty years.

Adam's hand is on my cheek, and when he leans down I know he's going to kiss me...and I know it will be wonderful. The sun warms my back and his lips warm my heart and suddenly I'm a woman with options.

I pull back and look at him, drink in this up-close-and-personal view of his vibrancy and good-ness and youth.

"Adam, I can't do this."

"I know you're separated, Beth."

"I'm still married, and to women of my generation that means something."

"I can wait."

"No...don't. I'm not going to dangle you while I make up my mind what to do about Howard. You're too fine, and I love and respect your grandparents too much."

"Does this mean my band can't play your music?"

"Indeed *not!* I want your band to debut 'Lonesome Blues.' I want to be in the front seat applauding."

"How about at the podium with roses?"

"That'll do, too." When I lean over to kiss his cheek I feel a contentment I haven't felt in a very long time. "Take care of yourself, Adam Price."

"You, too, Beth."

I can feel him watching as I walk away. There's a satisfaction in knowing he wants me that has nothing to do with sex and everything to do with being a woman, complete.

When I get home I make a nice chicken salad with pecans and grapes, a standard favorite from my Junior League days, and then go onto the front porch with Rufus.

"I have a lot of decisions to make here, old boy." He thumps his tail and I reach down to pat his big head. "It's nice to have a man who agrees with everything I say."

While I eat I watch a new moon rise in the deepening sky. This is a beautiful place. I wish I could share it with my family. I miss them. I miss Howard.

It doesn't seem right that we haven't talked. It's as if he and I have been on a luxury cruise for thirty years, and when the ship finally sank we jumped into separate lifeboats and drifted off in different directions. Why didn't one of us throw the other a lifeline?

After all these years you'd think at least one of us would take the initiative.

The frothing of waves against the shore look like

the edges of a white eyelet petticoat, and their lovely phosphorescence draws me toward the water with Rufus at my heels. Kicking off my sandals I wade along the shoreline and watch as the waves wash away my footprints.

The pull of the moon is strong, not only on the tides, but on me, and I find a perch on a small dune then lift my face toward the heavens. It's a clear night, and the sky is brilliant with stars.

Howard and I used to stargaze when we were courting. One evening he surprised me by saying, "Did you know that the stars are actually different colors?"

"They all look the same from here, and I guess I just took for granted that they were."

"A really good telescope shows stars that are a gem-quality blue and red. There are orange and yellow ones, too. The yellow dwarf stars have a life span of ten thousand million years, but the hotter, more brilliant ones live only a hundred million years."

I'm just a little blip on the cosmic radar. No matter what happens in my life, the moon, the sun and the myriad galaxies will endure.

I wonder if Howard is looking at the stars tonight, and if he's feeling the same thing I am: fleeting and impermanent. Compared to a star, we have an extremely short life span. Knowing that, wouldn't you think we'd try to get it right?

I dust the beach sand off my shorts, put on my sandals and walk back to the cottage with Rufus at my side.

Starting tomorrow, I'm going to try to get it right.

CHAPTER 24

"Can a stick-in-the-mud become
a man of mystery?"

—Howard

Here I am going after Beth again. Wouldn't you
think a man would have to do this only once in his
lifetime? If I keep thinking along those lines, I'll work
myself into another deep depression—I've been doing
that a lot lately—and then I'll never know if Beth and
I could have made it.

The fact is, I went off half-cocked in Pensacola and
she was right to leave again. Nothing changed when
we got home except the color of our bedroom walls.
I'll have to admit that dark pinkish color is not bad.
At least you notice it. First thing I see when I wake
up every morning is the way those walls look like the
sunrise, the kind that's soft and pinkish and leaves you
feeling as if you've jump-started a good day.

Well, actually it's the second thing I see. The first is Elizabeth's empty pillow.

The gas gauge on my car shows half-empty, so when I see an Exxon station on the outskirts of Meridian I pull in to fill up. One of the differences between Elizabeth and me is that I always drive off the top of the tank and she drives off the bottom.

I used to think it was cute, even when she got stranded that Christmas Eve at the mall and I had to rush out with a gas can so she could get to a service station. Then my fond amusement switched to irritation. And now... I don't know. I'm leaning more toward acceptance than anything.

While I'm still standing by my car with the gas nozzle in the tank, my cell phone goes off. Well, let it ring. I've got my hands full. Both literally and figuratively. Besides, it can't be all that important. It won't be Elizabeth because she hasn't called since she left, and Lucille knows to call me only in a dire emergency. And if it's Kate she'll call back.

Anyhow, I don't want to talk to her right now. I don't want her to know what I'm doing until I have something to report.

Maybe I'll call tomorrow afternoon. By then I should know the lay of the land in Ocean Springs. Or, knowing Elizabeth, maybe I won't. Unpredictability is one of her most maddening qualities…and one of her greatest charms.

When I go in to pay for the gas I encounter one of those chatty people behind the checkout counter, a burly man with *Ralph* embroidered on his shirt pocket.

"You pullin' a big load, I see."

"Yes."

"Mighty big, from the looks of it."

He's fishing, hoping I'll tell him what's in the trailer behind my car, but I'm not in the business of airing my family's laundry in public. Unlike Elizabeth who can spend ten minutes in a public restroom with a perfect stranger and share her entire family history. Furthermore, she comes out knowing everything about the person from sixth grade on. Often Elizabeth ends up dragging her home for a hot meal and a bath and some free psychiatric advice. From me, naturally.

I press my credit card in Ralph's hand and he stands there awhile, hoping I'll open up, but when I don't he goes on and does his job. Thank the good Lord.

On the way to the car the stars catch me unaware, and I stand in the middle of the parking lot staring like an old fool. Here's the crazy thing about stars: they always remind me of Elizabeth.

Life is excruciatingly dull without her.

Feeling misty-eyed, I get back in the car then have to sit behind the wheel awhile before my vision clears.

Back on Highway 45 South I turn on the radio for company. They're playing some kind of country song with guitars and tear-jerking lyrics sung in a twangy voice. Elizabeth always sings along. She has a clear, true voice that's better than some of the recording artists. She could have been famous if she'd pursued a career in entertainment, and I used to marvel that she chose plain, simple me instead of bright lights and big cities.

I listen closely to the words. They're repetitive and not hard to pick out, and when I start singing I startle myself. If only Elizabeth could hear me now. I'm not half-bad. Maybe I'll take up singing in the shower. Maybe I'll take up a lot of daring new habits.

If things go well in Ocean Springs.

The traffic's light this time of evening, and if I can hold this steady pace I'll be there before Elizabeth's bedtime. I wonder what she'll say when she sees me.

I wonder if she'll even let me in.

As I reach Laurel, the traffic's getting heavier. I've made it in record time, and I'm certainly not going to break speed to answer that dratted cell phone, which has started ringing again. Let it ring. Let 'er rip. My new philosophy. Be in the moment. That's what Jack Warner said.

"Howard, you've got to quit doing so much planning for the future and live in the moment. Hell, man, life's passing you by."

This is the same advice I give my patients, in more refined language of course, so why couldn't I see it for myself? That just goes to show that even normal, well-adjusted adults benefit from an occasional session with a good psychiatrist who knows his business.

My phone finally quits ringing, and I keep driving south, closing in on Hattiesburg, which is only eighty-five miles from the Mississippi Gulf Coast.

Lord, this town brings back memories. The second year we were married, Elizabeth and I came down here for one of my state conventions. I knew from the beginning I shouldn't try to mix business with pleasure, but in those lusty years we could hardly bear to be apart.

We'd sneaked out of a boring cocktail party early and then had one of our own in our motel room. Just the two of us. Not at all boring. Around 2:00 a.m. Elizabeth pranced out the door in her underwear before I could stop her.

"Ta, ta. Gotta get ice."

She was tanked. Loaded on too much booze and too much sex.

Fortunately, I grabbed my robe before I went after her because I was buck naked. Too late, I heard the lock catch behind me. Do you think I had a key? Not a chance.

When I went around the corner and found her at the ice machine, she laughed her head off.

"I'll just go down to the office to ask for a key."

I had to grab her or she'd have pranced into the front office in her underwear. And of course, I wasn't about to go down there in nothing but a robe. We ended up hunkered down by the ice machine, spooned together in my robe, and I'll have to say it was one of the most erotic experiences of my life. Enhanced, I think, by the chance of getting caught.

An early-morning custodian let us in at five with his skeleton key. I slipped him a twenty, and asked him not to tell, and so far as I know he never did. Or else he told and my colleagues played the ultimate joke on me and kept it a secret all these years.

− If I got locked out again would I still wait on a hard balcony instead of getting the key? I don't know. Seems as if I've been hunkered down for a long time doing without both my wife and the key to our once-cozy life.

The trick, of course, is not to use the same key after the lock has been changed. I've already started a search for a new business partner, which will give me the time to do the traveling that Elizabeth has always wanted. And if she's dead-set on staying in Ocean Springs, then I'll move my practice. I can make a good living, no matter where I am.

What I can't do is make a good marriage without Elizabeth.

My cell phone rings again, and this time I'm on a straight, lonely stretch of I-49 so I answer.

"Howard? Finally, I've got you."

"Elizabeth?"

"Yes, it's me. How are you?"

To tell or not to tell. I'd counted on the element of surprise and her ingrained Southern manners to ensure that I had a bed to sleep in tonight, but maybe it's time to impress her. Let her know the lengths a man will go to in order to keep the things that are worth having.

Besides, didn't Jack Warner say, "Just open up, Howard. Express your feelings"?

"I'm lonely and I'm missing you and I'm headed your way."

I hear her catch her breath. Finally she asks, "Where are you?"

"In the middle of nowhere, sixty miles from your cottage."

"I can't believe this."

"Are you pleasantly surprised or otherwise?"

"I don't know yet, Howard. It all depends."

Lately I've hated it when Elizabeth is imprecise, but Jack helped me see that not every little thing in life is cut-and-dried. To be fair, how can I expect her to make a spur-of-the-moment decision about emotions tied up with thirty years of baggage?

"Elizabeth, I'm hoping for more, but all I'm asking is that you give me a chance to talk. Okay?"

"Fair enough. See you later, alligator."

"After a while, crocodile."

Her sassy way of saying goodbye gives me hope, and I press down on the accelerator, testing the speed limits, clipping off the miles that are taking me southward, a Greek bearing gifts.

When I pull into the familiar driveway—so many Christmases and Thanksgivings spent here, so many summer holidays romping on the beach—the porch light flips on, and Elizabeth comes out in a short white cotton robe with a pink-lined hood. Her feet are bare and she's got her arms around herself in that stance she always takes when she's not sure whether she's making a good impression.

I park in the two-car garage, then dawdle a minute, drinking in the sight of my wife's bare legs and her scrubbed face. She's never looked better to me.

But even with performance-guaranteed Viagra in my pocket I'm not going to walk right in and haul her off to the bedroom. Been there, done that. It didn't work in Pensacola, and I'm not fixing to court failure by repeating my mistakes in Ocean Springs.

Instead I walk onto the porch and greet her casually.

"Hello, Elizabeth."

"Long time, no see, Howard." She tucks her hands into the full sleeves of her robe and rocks back and forth on her feet. I haven't seen Elizabeth this shy with me since the early days of our courtship. Is this a good sign or a bad?

"I've brought you something," I say.

"I can see that. It's an awfully large trailer, Howard."

"It has to be. Your baby grand's inside."

"You brought my piano?"

She never could hide her emotions. They race across her face now: joy then hope then puzzlement.

Of course, she's putting it all together and coming up with the conclusion that this is a prelude to divorce, the separation of belongings. I hasten to put her mind at ease.

"I'll get the local piano movers to come out here in the morning and get it inside. Wherever you are, Elizabeth, I want you to have your baby grand."

"You mean, if I decide to go back to Tupelo, you'd haul it two hundred and fifty miles north again?"

"I would."

"And if I changed my mind and decided to move down here without you, you'd bring it back?"

"Yes."

"Oh my goodness…"

Crying and laughing at the same time, she launches herself at me before I can brace myself, and both of us tumble backward. Fortunately, the porch swing is behind us, and I manage to catch hold and land in a heap without breaking both our necks.

We squirm around trying to find the right fit for the swing's seat and each other. When we finally settle back, Elizabeth's as flustered as a schoolgirl.

"Let's sit out here where it's cool, Howard. Unless you're tired from the long drive and want to go inside."

Does she mean to her bed or the sofa? It's too early

to bring up sleeping arrangements. I'd sit here in this swing even if I were falling asleep in my tracks.

"This is fine."

"There's a lot of unresolved stuff between us, Howard."

"I know. And believe me, Elizabeth, I'm trying." When I tell her about my search for a new associate, she nods. It's not much, certainly not the reaction I'd expected, but as Aunt Bonnie Kathleen was fond of saying, *Rome wasn't built in a day.*

"That means we can do some traveling, Elizabeth…if you want to."

"I'm going to go back to work, Howard."

Oh God, she's found a job and she's fixing to tell me she's moving down here and I can just get in my car and go home. Nodding is all I feel like doing, but part of our problem was lack of communication so I wrack my brain to think of the best thing to say.

If I say, *That's fine with me*—and it is—she'll think I'm acting as if she needs my permission. And if I say, *I'm glad*, she'll think I'm judging her for not working all those years.

Great-granny's nightgown. The problem with being a psychiatrist is that everybody expects you to say the perfect thing all the time.

"Tell me about it, Elizabeth."

Her smile is my reprieve, and I listen quietly while she tells me about her blues songs and her discovery that she wants to be a band director again.

"Just think, Howard. I can use a lot of my own songs this time, and maybe I'll publish them so other bands can play them."

"That's wonderful." And it is. But here comes the hard part. "Does that mean you're staying down here, Elizabeth?"

"I don't know."

Well…Jack told me this wouldn't be easy. I set the swing in motion and we sit side by side like an ordinary couple on a typical moonlit night.

Maybe everything is illusion.

"Beth?"

"Hmm?"

"I know I acted an ass with Jenny, and I know I have to fix it. But she's always seemed to be more yours than mine, lively and free-spirited and self-assured in a way that I didn't quite understand."

I run my hands across the top of my head, vividly aware of my baldness and my inadequacy.

"I guess I don't quite know how to deal with her," I add. "In spite of my ninety-dollar-an-hour fees."

The swing rocks on, but the silence between us seems more comfortable now.

"Howard, I'm finally fixing things with Kate. You can do it with Jenny."

Elizabeth pats my knee and I nearly jump off the swing. At last I'm seeing Elizabeth in a new way, not as merely my wife but as a woman in her own right.

"Why don't we go inside?" she says. "You can sleep in my old room or I'll put some blankets on Aunt Bonnie Kathleen's couch."

"The same old couch with the cabbage roses?"

"They are awful, aren't they?"

It's nice that the last thing we do together before we go to our separate beds is laugh.

By the time Elizabeth gets up, I've already called the movers to come over and unload the baby grand. She's like a little girl running around in her yellow shorts with her spiky red hair.

The hair grows on you.

And the personality... Frankly, it's what I miss most about Elizabeth. All of us have a child inside, but she's one of the few people I know who lets hers out to play. Maybe I did briefly when I put on that god-awful Hawaiian shirt in Pensacola, and maybe if

I did more of that I might be more the kind of man she seems to need. Fun-loving. That's not a bad thing.

It's nearly lunch by the time the movers leave.

"Is Jim's Seafood Shack still in business?" I ask, and when she nods, we head downtown.

She orders oysters.

"The first time I ever saw you, you were eating oysters."

"Howard...you remembered."

"I remember a lot of things, Elizabeth. The way you lit up like a Christmas tree when your band kids performed."

"Do you want to hear my new music?"

"Yes. I've missed hearing you play your baby grand."

I reach for her hand when we go to the car, and it feels so good I wonder why I ever had to be prompted.

Back at the cottage I fall in love with my wife all over again. She plays with a passion that sucks me in, draws me closer. When I lean against her back and put my hand on her shoulder, she falters, then stops.

"Howard?"

"Sorry." I step back, amazed at my reaction, even without Viagra. "I didn't mean to do that."

She swivels toward me with two bright red spots on her cheeks.

"If I take you into my bedroom will you think it means you're home free? Because it won't, you know. I haven't made up my mind about you, Howard Martin."

"I know. But I've got my mind made up about you. That counts twice as much."

"I don't want to think about math right now."

"Neither do I."

Here we are making out like sixteen-year-olds in the middle of the afternoon. Sweat drenches the sheets and every inch of our skin, and still I'm as pumped up as a Kentucky thoroughbred at stud.

"Wait." Panting, Elizabeth lifts herself on one elbow. "Not that I don't like this…I do, I do! But how do you turn that thing off? You're driving a Model-T instead of Thunderbird."

"You're no Model-T. Guaranteed."

I can't keep my hands off her. Diving under the covers I begin to suck her toes and then make my way upward.

"Howard…wait, wait…what if we dance? Maybe that will take the edge off."

She bounds out of bed and the sight of her cute butt disappearing around the corner only exacerbates my condition. I round the corner after her just as she puts on one of those slow, classical pieces she's so fond of. You'd think after all these years of living with her, I'd know the names, but I don't.

That's just one more reason why I need Elizabeth. How will I keep the music straight without her?

Pulling her close, I whisper, "You sure know how to make it hard on a man."

"Good grief, Howard." She giggles as I awkwardly two-step her around the room. "Would it help if I put a sack on my head?"

"Wrong body part," I say, but she prances off anyway, as giddy as a teenager.

When she comes back, she's wearing this Winn-Dixie paper sack over her head with holes cut out for her eyes, nose and mouth. Around her waist she's hung several strings of faded fake chili peppers.

"I like your hula skirt, woman. Let's hula."

I'm swinging that thing like there's no tomorrow, and Elizabeth's prancing around me like a filly in heat.

Grabbing Aunt Bonnie Kathleen's rose afghan, she swings it in front of me like a matador's cape.

"Olé! Olé!"

I never knew laughing and cavorting could be this liberating.

"Howard. Wait. Did you hear something?"

"Nothing except all this blood pumping through me."

"I'm serious. Shhh. Listen."

Now I hear it, a tapping at the front door and a voice I know all too well.

"Mom?"

Kate. Good Lord.

I jerk the afghan out of Elizabeth's hand and she shoves me toward the bedroom.

"Hide. Put on some clothes. And for Pete's sake…" She gestures toward my pride and joy. "Do something about that thing."

CHAPTER 25

"Getting it right."

—Beth

The shock of hearing Kate on my front porch is so great I don't even take time to remove the chili peppers. I just throw on my robe and fling open the door.

"Nana, Nana." Bonnie catapults into my arms and I bury my face in her neck inhaling the wonderful scent of baby powder and innocence.

"We wanted to surprise you," Kate says.

"It's a wonderful surprise."

All of a sudden Howard's planted solidly beside me, wearing his slacks and shirt, thank goodness.

"Daddy? I didn't know you were here."

She always runs to her daddy, which is natural since I left Howard in charge of the important parts of her upbringing. But learning she didn't know he was here means I'm closing the long-standing gap between us, and I am unutterably grateful.

"Maybe I have a few surprises up my sleeve, too."

I haven't seen Howard this jovial since he found out I was pregnant with Kate. As for the surprises... they were definitely not up his sleeve.

"Come in and I'll get you some tea. We've had a long walk on the beach and your mother was just fixing to hop into the shower."

He was born competent. In moments of crisis, he's the one who will step forward to take care of the necessary details. The incident that sticks in my mind is last New Year's Eve when we came upon a three-car pileup. While everybody else ran around, panicked, Howard called the ambulance and the police, then found coats strewn around the frozen ground and covered everybody before the emergency personnel arrive.

Of course, he's never lied before, that amazes me. Even better, knowing he did it to protect me, thrills me.

I excuse myself and head to the shower with Rufus at my heels, and as I shuck off my robe and my chili peppers I tell the dog, "That's one of the most amazing things he's ever done, Rufus."

With the water pounding my body I realize I've always counted on his ability to remain levelheaded. Even when I was in Sedona, furious at him about Jenny, I knew deep down he would take care of the details of my staying behind and his going home.

And without fanfare. Which is also Howard's way. He's never been one to rant and carry on. A blessing, really, when you think of all the bickering couples you see in airports and restaurants and even the aisles of grocery stores where they'll argue about something as insignificant as the kind of lettuce to buy.

Now when I head back to the living room, I'm grateful Howard's back.

"Where's Rick?" I ask, as I sit down.

The minute I do, Bonnie hops in my lap, and I'm a grandmother in a rocking chair. But I'm also a lush, just-loved woman feeling sexy and demure and shy and bold all at the same time.

"He had to come down for a conference in Pensacola, so I decided to bring Bonnie over here. He'll join us Tuesday, if that's all right."

"Of course."

I try to read between the lines and see the state of her marriage, but all I see is a beautiful young woman with a smile on her face. A good sign, I think.

"I have something I want you to see. Bonnie, sweetheart, stand up and let Nana see your dress."

It's pink batiste with tiny tucking along the bodice with delicate lace, feminine and Victorian-looking.

"It's my design. I'm launching Kate's for Kids in October."

She grew wings after all. I am overwhelmed, and Howard steps into the breach.

He puts his hand on Kate's shoulder, a solid, capable hand with squared-off fingers and a sprinkling of hair along the back.

"I'm proud of you, Kate. You're talented, like your mother, and I'm glad to see you stepping out and taking risks."

A part of me that has been standing back for months holding its breath suddenly relaxes. I've always loved Howard's hands. Maybe I've always loved him, even when I wanted to strangle him with one of his ultraconservative, ugly pinstripe ties. If it took leaving home to make me see that, the flight was worth the drama.

We have supper on the porch, and afterward walk along the beach, Rufus trailing along, barking, and Bonnie laughing in Howard's arms until she falls asleep.

It's one of those moments you want to press between the pages of an album and keep until the faded
yellow pages fall apart.

When we go back inside, Kate says good-night and
goes to my old bedroom while Howard and I stand
shoulder to shoulder beside the baby grand piano.

"I can sleep on the cabbage roses," he says.

"No." I take his hand and lead him to my bedroom.

"It was quite a day, toots."

"It was."

Amazing, really, when you consider how far we
had to travel to find each other again.

The chili peppers are flung across the bedspread
where I left them. When I reach to move them so I
can turn back the covers, Howard stops me.

"Let me." He hangs them on the bedpost, while I
watch, suddenly shy.

"Did you bring your pajamas?"

"No. I don't need them."

I have to tamp down my elation. After all, it's only
a pair of pajamas, a small concession. There are still
lots of unresolved issues between us, including Jenny.

We climb into bed on opposite sides, and he
reaches out and draws me into his arms. Everything
about him is familiar to me—the smell of his after-

shave, the feel of his beard stubble against my cheek, the angle and fit of his bones between his neck and shoulder—familiar and yet brand-new. This time he's present in the bed really holding me, finally seeing me.

And I hope I see him, too. I really do.

Howard reaches between us and links his fingers through mine.

"Does this mean we're okay, Elizabeth?"

"I don't know, yet. But it's a good start."

They were twin sisters with nothing in common…

Until they teamed up on a cross-country
adventure to find their younger sibling.
And ended up figuring out that, despite
buried secrets and wrong turns, all roads
lead back to family.

Sisters

by Nancy Robards Thompson

Hearing that her husband
had owned a cottage in England
was a surprise. But the truly
shocking news was what
she would find there.

Determined to discover more about the cottage
her deceased husband left her, Marjorie Maitland
travels to England to visit the property—and
ends up uncovering secrets from the past that
might just be the key to her future.

The English Wife

by Doreen Roberts

Available June 2006
TheNextNovel.com

HN47

HARLEQUIN®
Next™

Is reality better than fantasy?

When her son leaves for college, Lauren
realizes it is time to start a new life for herself.
After a series of hilarious wrong turns,
she lands a job decorating department-store
windows. Is the "perfect" world she creates
in the windows possible to find in real life?
Ready or not, it's time to find out!

Window Dressing

by Nikki Rivers

◆ HARLEQUIN®

Next™

HN48

Available June 2006
TheNextNovel.com

REQUEST YOUR FREE BOOKS!

2 FREE NOVELS TO INTRODUCE YOU TO OUR BRAND-NEW LINE!

NeXt ™

There's the life you planned. And there's what comes next.

Life is full of hope.

Facing a family crisis, Melinda and
her husband are forced to look
at their lives and end up learning
what is really important.

Falling Out
of Bed

by
Mary Schramski